Eronica Unbound

Also by Scarlett Vaughn

Novels
Eronica Unbound

Collections
The Binding Realm: Collected Stories

Also by Scott P. Vaughn

Novels
Shards of Destiny – Hero-Lore Book I

Crimson Cutlass and Chameleon

Collections
Warbirds of Mars – Stories of the Fight!

Comics
Autumn Moon

Warbirds of Mars: The Golden Age

Eronica Unbound

Scarlett Vaughn

Illustrated by Scott P. Vaughn

Copyright ©2023 by Paperstreet Ent., LLC
All rights reserved.
Originally e-published as *Slaves of Shebwai: Eronica Unbound* in 2010 by Phaze Books.
Cover Artwork and illustrations by Scott P. Vaughn. Used with permission.

Visit Scarlett Vaughn on the World Wide Web at:
www.paperstreetent.com

Visit illustrator Scott P. Vaughn on the World Wide Web at:
www.vaughn-media.com

Warning: This is a fantasy tale of bondage, sex and erotic romance. This story was written to unlock your darkest fantasies and innermost desires; it is not your mother's bodice-ripper. It contains a confident heroine in both consensual and reluctant sexual situations, including pirates, harems, an auction, a powerful Sultan, fellatio, cunnilingus, rough sex, group sex, S&M, a shape-shifting mage and more. All of the sexual descriptions found in this book are very explicit in nature. It is erotica intended for open-minded readers over 18 years of age. Read at your own risk.

Prologue

Eronica watched the sea, reveling in the way the water lapped at her toes like a patient lover, drawing her in. The wind blew in from across the harbor. It whipped Eron's long brunette hair around her face, the humidity making it stick to her skin. She imagined that the breeze had traveled up from the lesser kingdoms, thousands of miles across the ocean just to cool the sweat channeling down the hollow between her full breasts and then permeate through the layers of her gown to brush her stomach and thighs.

The 'Sea of Blue Longing' called to her, hoping to bind her to it and drown her in its depths. In truth, Eron reflected, it was no different than her past loves; they all wanted to control her and make her their own possessions. The others—those few lovers at court she had taken since leaving the *Chateau De Shaines*—she'd had little time to give in to them. Her own aspirations had always pulled her away, ultimately leaving her feeling unfulfilled. This one—the sea—*this* she was obligated to go to. Eron had to give herself willingly to the expanse of blue and the storms it brought, and she knew she must let it become her master to do with her as it pleased. Like the sea, she would be subject to fate's whims and trust that she could come out safe on the other side if she were to complete the task she had been given. A task only she could carry out.

She felt a hand gently touch her shoulder, and Eron turned away from the forebodingly serene scene to find Corine smiling at her. The maidservant was younger than the Lady Eronica's twenty-five years, but no less lovely. The pretty redhead with her thin frame and perky breasts was a striking sight in the failing daylight. "My Lady," the servant said in a lilting voice. "Your presence is requested at the harbormaster's house."

Eron looked up the beach to the crowded harbor just beyond the rocky peninsula. Her king and the task that he had given her were waiting in secret at that boathouse. This was what her skills, patriotism, and ambitions had brought her to. Eron sighed, picking up her shoes from the wet sand and set off to get her final pep talk before embarking on her harrowing journey.

My Lady will not tell me what it is that is bothering her so," Corine said as they passed the ship that they would both soon board.

The wooden timbers that made up the merchant vessel *The Black Kettle* creaked as the wind rocked her against the mooring peer. The sun was nearly set, and the twin moons were already rising in the north. At least the sky had been briefly red before the darkness fell, Eron thought. "And yet you still insist you will come along," she chided her servant.

"You say that our training at the *Chateau* will become the only means of our survival. That is how we met, My Lady," Corine said, still sounding strangely happy and upbeat to Eron's ears. The serving girl was referring to their time together at the training school for concubines, dominants and submissives. "Like there, we will need each other in order to cope. Besides," she grinned, taking her mistress's hand, "I like rough seafaring men almost as much as I like a woman's touch."

"I hope so," Eronica warned as they came at last to the harbormaster's house. "We are both going to need those skills before this trip is finished."

Corine suddenly pulled her aside to the shadows, where the house windows could not see them. She pulled her mistress close, so that their faces were almost touching, and whispered. "I'm frightened, Eron."

Eron ran her fingers down the girl's cheek as she stared into the pools of her friend's eyes. "I know," she told her, but refrained from admitting how scared she was. Instead she kissed Corine, lightly at first, but soon the fear and excitement had them both groping for each other's flesh despite the heavy drapery of their dresses. Thoughts of the two friends' time together in consolation at the Chateau made Eron blush, as if those memories were somehow more potent than the engaging kiss she was now subject to. Their tongues mingled and the sweet flavor of the girl's mouth made Eron's nipples erect.

Just as Corine was beginning to tug at the shoulder hem of her Lady's gown, the Harbormaster exited the front door of his home and passed them in the dark, never seeing them. The women watched in stunned silence for a moment before giggling nervously together and rearranging their appearances to enter the house.

Eron stopped to take one look back at the city that had been her home of the past few years. The fading light and the mist of the sea would not allow even that final sunset. It only afforded her the sight of the old Harbormaster boarding the very vessel she was about to embark for her mission.

"Come," she commanded her servant. "There is still much to do this night, and our courage must hold out." Smoothing down her dress, Eron smiled at Corine and then led the way towards the decking that curved elegantly to the boathouse's front doors. She took one large breath, and then reached out for the handles to let herself in.

Chapter 1

Within the large but modestly decorated wooden home's foyer two soldiers waited. Eron knew that they were royal guards in disguise, so she left Corine with one while following the other deeper into the house. She studied the back of the man's breastplate and then the backside of his breeches as he walked, realizing with a pang of regret that her sexuality had been awakened, as much by Corine's kiss as by the fear and power that surrounded her now. Resisting the urge to comment on the long-sword slung at the handsome guard's hip, Eron bit the inside of her cheek and silenced herself against the coming meeting.

In an office of deep oak, behind a desk littered with the brass tools of ocean navigation, sat the most prevailing man in the Five Kingdoms. Henrick, monarch of Capriana, was an attractive if slightly overweight man. His beard had been peppered with gray in recent years and he had let his hair grow, much to the chagrin of his wife. His robes were of the finest weave of gold and red.

King Henrick II was by definition the most powerful man in the world, as his seat held sway over the lesser, smaller kingdoms. This man and the land that he ruled stood for the things that Eron had come to believe in, so in a strange way she loved him. It was neither a father figure nor lover she saw in him, but an ideal within herself that the king represented. She had been so star-struck the first time they had met, but their relations had always been of Capriana business, which sometimes included pleasure. Ultimately it had all resulted in respect and what Eron called friendship, and it had given her position and power, though in truth she longed for further stability even in a land as fertile as hers.

"Eronica," the guard quietly announced, "Lady of Tibeth."

Eronica bowed and her King smiled, excusing the guard with a simple wave of his hand.

"Beautiful, as always, Lady Eronica," the King said. He openly appraised the ample portion of cleavage that her bodice afforded him, then sat back to study her from behind steepled fingers. "Eron," he began, dropping any pretense of protocol between them for their conversation. "You still have this chance to stay and not involve yourself in such dangerous matters. You could always become the lover of myself and the queen."

He offered it up with seriousness and a welcome nature that nearly shook the Lady's resolve. The King was giving her one last chance to say 'no,' she knew, but Eron was aware of the importance of this mission and the trust he was secretly placing in her for the sake of his realm.

Capriana was the largest and richest of the Kingdoms, and the ornate marble castles and cities and the richly carved woods of its ports and towns could attest to that. Henrick's monarchy had birthed, built and expanded since antiquity, and the line of king's could still be traced to Henrick's blood. The First Kingdom enjoyed the imported riches of the other four it had settled as well, leaving few within Eron's homeland in any true state of poverty. Tragedy could befall anyone, as well she knew, but still she had been able to rise to a point where—had she chosen—she could have become the concubine of the King himself. As the Queen still lived and commanded Henrick's attentions, Eronica passed on this idea. But still, she had risen to a state of importance, and for all it had given her she would defend her nation and its ideals to the death.

Now a shadow from the lower Provinces loomed over Lady Eronica's beloved homeland. The fleets and armies of the province of Shebwai—that strange desert land far to the south—threatened Henrick's dominion. Already the Sultan of Shebwai's greed for conquest had swallowed two Kingdoms: Granelayde and the Grey Isles. Shebwai's power had consumed them and enslaved each quickly, yet so much of that powerful desert nation was still a mystery to Eron. She had heard tales of its debauchery and cruelty: That women and men both were made unwilling slaves to the nobility or the Sultan, and that torture and foul magic was practiced with regularity. The Sultan lived in opulence, conjuring black spells with his necromancer in a bid to rule the world while his slaves were forced to pleasure them both. The whole place sounded prickly and dangerous. Despite this, she felt a strange attraction to its mystery and peril, as well as the wonder that its treasures must truly hold to keep men of such power there in oasis palaces surrounded by a wasteland and a growing army.

Eron had to push such darkly enticing thoughts from her mind before the King might notice the quickening of her breath. She realized that a moment of silence had passed while she had pondered her fate, and she became determined to look as well as sound resolute and brave.

"My Lady?"

"Thank you, Your Majesty, but I have already given you my word. Just as I promised myself long ago that I would find a husband of importance to take as my own." Eron smiled as warmly as she could muster for her King, but the butterflies in her stomach were positively buzzing now. It was a sensation that she had been trying to ignore until now, but it was impossible to do so any longer. As with all important decisions, it felt somehow wrong at that moment when you actually signed the dotted line. Eron suddenly wished desperately that she could sit down or loosen her corset, but protocol demanded otherwise until the King commanded as such.

"And we thank you for your perseverance, My Lady. When you return, you can name your prize. The simple 'Lady' need not be your title much longer."

"Yes, Your majesty."

The King's countenance became serious at last. "What you are about to undertake is treacherous in the extreme. I need not remind you that there is always the possibility that you will not even make it to Shebwai—that pirates with no loyalties still prowl the waters you shall be crossing. Should you not be picked up before reaching what is your documented, official destination, make your way to Shebwai however you must. You will have only a limited time to find your way into the Sultan of Shebwai's graces before my agents make your escape route apparent to you." He shook his head, but told her, "I admire you, Lady Eronica. This is a very brave thing you are doing. I am not even certain that I agree with your choosing this task. As I have told my spellweaver, so much could go wrong."

"Your Majesty, I understand the risks. It will work out, you will see." Eron looked up, smiling genuinely for but a moment at Henrick III, Prince and only heir, as he entered through a side door. She continued, "If your harbormaster has done his work properly, then my ship will drift into waters smart merchants avoid, knowing that the privateers there are in the employ of the Sultan. Within a week I'll be on the block, and my beauty and skill will put me on our enemy's lap within a month." Even as she said it with what she hoped was confidence, Eron thought the words were strange and hollow in her own ears. How could she take on this task? What was she doing? Putting herself in this enormous amount of danger was insane! But she kept her chin up, said the words, impressed her royal masters, and prepared to march out of the office in glorious homage to her duty as a Lady of Capriana, the most civilized nation in the world.

"This is a risky venture," The King said finally, "and we both sacrifice much. Even though the *Black Kettle* is a foreign ship, I am loathe to do this to her crew. With luck, they will escape death and simply be put off and robbed by whatever ship meets you all out there. But you must not concern yourself with such matters; just do your duty to the crown, and you will survive this and help to end the tyranny that threatens this nation and her people." Eron nodded, swallowing down the lump of pride and fear that threatened to bring tears to her eyes or bile to her mouth; she knew not which. King Henrick II rose from his seat and kissed Eron's cheeks, bidding her farewell. Eron turned on her heel to leave, and it was all she could do to stay balanced on her shaky feet.

Even as the door closed behind her she was again contemplating what had led her to this task. "Mother, Father," she whispered to the heavens. "I only want to honor you and the legacy you gave me. Please understand."

Eron's parents had been rich, but their deaths had left her orphaned at the age of fourteen. Fiercely independent, she had used her relatively meager titles to associate herself with those who could get her into the palace. Whispers here, advice there, and blind desire for elevation no matter what the cost had made her decide to attend at the *Chateau*, so that she would be a more appealing prize when her time within the palace came. Eron spent two years locked away in a den of indulgence and expensive tastes, both carnally and esthetically. Then, with her faithful new servant Corine in tow, she had left, rising quickly from the depths of the *Chateau De Shaines* to the center of her realm. But with the King's palace and the proximity to royalty had come knowledge and time-consuming experience. Suddenly Eron was part of a world where the Prince himself was within her grasp, but she was too busy doing her part for King and country for either party to notice until it was too late. The Prince had become arranged in the last month, and as usual Eron was left doing the paperwork and spending nights with lesser men with smaller ambitions and mundane desires. As always, Eronica wanted so much more.

Eron's mind was frozen with the staggering prospects now laid out before her. She let her feet carry her forward, placing one step before the other as though in a trance.

"Eron!" The Prince caught her in the halls leading back to where Corine waited. Turning her bodily he pinned her to the wall, letting his size keep her from escaping any longer. Eron gasped when his mouth came down on hers. They had never before had the chance to kiss, but she was too nervous and he too impatient to gauge the chemistry of the joining. Besides, Eron thought, he was a betrothed man now.

"Your Majesty, please," she said, turning her head away. It only left her earlobe open to attack. She tried not to smile, then pushed him away at last. "Please," she said again.

"You would deny us?" Prince Henrick III asked, his blue eyes serious and scrutinizing. He was ever so much more handsome and less boyish in this close proximity. "I may never see you again."

"And *now* you want me?" she admonished. "You have had years to make your feelings known. This is not a land of secrets and scandals, Your Majesty. You had your chance, if I may be so bold."

"And I was always too afraid of your beauty." He sounded genuine enough. Even then, Lady Eronica was not royalty, and therefore could never have married him. Perhaps it had been she who had stayed away. "Now you're leaving."

"I'll be back," she promised. "Perhaps then you can take me as your lover for a time before I find some Duke to marry, but I'll not be your concubine, Majesty. I'm sorry."

The Prince calmed, but he was obviously disappointed and perhaps honestly worried for her. "And tonight?"

Eron bit off a loud, uneasy laugh. "Tonight? Tonight I need my sleep if I am to have any sea legs worth a damn tomorrow, Majesty." Enticed as she was by his offer, her mind screamed at her to let rest come before pleasure or duty, lest she no longer be able to stand. Eron smiled apologetically to him. "I would be so ill at ease, and if I drank my fears away, well, heaven and gods forefend what the consequences on the deck of that ship might be tomorrow."

They both laughed at that. After a brief quiet Henrick III said, "I don't know yet what mission it is my father sends you on. Perhaps he will tell me tomorrow, when you're gone." *Gods*, she thought, how long had he wanted her? How long had the king, a man who openly wanted her for himself, known and still sympathized with his son? "Just be careful, Lady," he said, "For all our sakes."

The Prince kissed Eron's hand, and reluctantly turned away.

Eron and Corine had been given a large bedroom for the night, high up in the Harbormaster's house. The night was growing late, considering they had to be up before the dawn, but Eron was entirely too rattled to sleep.

Corine was pouring a glass of wine, which the Lady tried to decline. "Take it," her friend said, placing it in her hand. "It's only a drink. It will calm your nerves."

Eron frowned but took the glass, sipping the red contents. It wasn't too dry, and had a light flowering that opened her tongue to new flavors. The bottle's label was a vintage she recognized as an expensive brand from the Valiende, in the Second Kingdom. The Harbormaster was obviously a man well off who enjoyed the finer things in life despite his grizzled looks. "Its good," she said, suddenly feeling melancholy.

Corine must have seen the lost look in her mistress's eyes as she stared over the glass. "Let's get you ready for bed, My Lady." She stood behind Eron and began unlacing the back of her bodice and skirts. Before Eron knew it, she was nearly nude and being sat on the edge of the old but comfortable bed in her stockings and thong, getting her hair undone. "There," Corine said with satisfaction, and then took a moment to remove her own dress. Eron watched as the girl's shift fell to the floor, leaving Corine naked except for her tiny socks and the black choker that denoted her as a servant. She smiled at her mistress when she saw the way she had been watched. She doused one oil lamp, giving the room an air of twilight. With a knowing smile cast over one naked shoulder, Corine batted her eyes seductively. "I thought that might get your attention," she said huskily, then playfully blew a stray wisp of red hair off of her nose.

Eron relaxed a little and reached for her friend. "You're too good to me."

"This I know, My Lady." Corine put her arms over her mistress's shoulders and then laughed when the older girl nuzzled her small yet firm breasts. She jiggled them back and forth slightly in Eron's face, giggling at her own silly act. Eron gave in with a loud sigh, expelling her worries through a breath, as they had both been taught at *Chateau De Shaines* what seemed like so long ago now. She laughed at her friend's attempts to cheer her up and snuggled the inviting flesh.

They fell to the bed together. Soon they were kissing each other deeply, wrapped in one another's arms and heating the cold bed's covers with their bodies. Eron luxuriated in the taste and soft rasp of Corine's tongue as it encircled hers. The kiss became long and wet, and soon small breathy sounds were escaping the less-experienced girl's mouth between moments of the kiss. Eron laughed again, pulling back to run her hands down the lithe girl's trembling body. Corine always was the more wanton one, giving herself into the moment so completely that it was almost funny. They were not lovers often, but they seemed to find each other like this in times of need, and Eron rarely declined.

"I know how you want it," Eron said as she grabbed her servant's hands aggressively. She held Corine's arms over her head with one hand while pinching one small pink nipple with the other. She rubbed the girl's body down with her own, letting their jutting peaks and hallowed hips nudge and slide alongside one another. Eron straddled Corine and pinched her flesh, never releasing her hands from her own grip.

The other girl could have easily wriggled free, but she liked being taken like this, so she kept her arms where her mistress had silently commanded. "Yes, My Lady," she breathed as Eron took Corine's wet, hard nipple into her mouth. "Yes, mistress! Take me, I am yours!"

"Alright," Eronica said with an evil smirk, "I shall." She reached down beside the bed where their gowns still sat, retaining the heat from the girls' bodies. She grasped the first yard of ribbon she could get her hands on and used it to secure Corine's hands to the bars of the bed's frame. As she worked at making the bonds tight, Eron worked her hips over her servant's face strategically. Corine did not need commanding; she reached out with her little tongue and began questing through the soft brown curls until she found the softest places nestled there. Corine's mouth claimed the velvety folds of Eron's quim, eliciting a moan at last. Eron reached down and grabbed her friend by the hair, pulling her face up further. "Lick it," she said, and moaned again.

Then there was a knock at the door.

Eronica and Corine froze, the blood in their veins chilling at the prospect of being found in another's house engaged scandal. Sexuality was an open subject in Capriana, to be sure, but this was still a compromising situation. Before Eronica could find voice enough to demand who might be interrupting her 'rest', she watched in horror as the door handle turned.

She had watched Corine lock that door!

Prince Henrick III stepped through the portal quickly and used the key in his hand to lock the door again, giving them both a smile. "Ladies," he said simply.

Eron sat atop her friend's chest, stunned and with mouth agape. Caught somewhere between embarrassment and enticement, she had no idea what to say.

"My gods," Corine gasped from glistening lips. "The Prince!" she whispered.

Henrick brought a finger to his upturned lips and winked. "No one need know."

Eronica dropped her shoulders with a sardonic look. "*We* know. With what right do you enter my rooms? My words in the hallway were somehow not enough to express my feelings to you?"

With a look heavenward, Henrick shrugged. "Do you forget your place, Lady Eronica?" he said with mock authority.

"I am on a mission for the King!" Eron exclaimed with shock.

"Not yet, you're not." He approached the bed. "I could leave if you wished, ladies. I would tell no one of what transpired here, one way or the other." He looked down, his blue eyes shadowed by his blonde locks. "Or I could stay, and we could all enjoy a moment of passing time. Capriana owes you that much for your services, even before they have been rendered."

Eron still kneeled there like a statue, her fists clenched as she stared back at her Prince. At last she looked down at her friend and gave her a quizzical glance.

But Corine was staring transfixed at the handsome Prince, never having had the chance to be this close to a man that Eron knew they both secretly desired. Corine was a servant, after all. That was the profession the *Chateau* had trained her for, and becoming the concubine of royalty was hardly something one of her class would turn away. "Let him stay," she whispered breathily—almost desperately.

"That's one vote in my favor," Henrick said, but there was victory in his eyes.

Eron unclenched her fist and held it out to him as an invitation. Henrick relaxed his powerful stature and took the outstretched hand just long enough to kiss it before he began to disrobe, dropping his rich garments to the rugs.

"Just tell me that the harbormaster or the King is not watching us through some secret porthole," Eron warned. She took in his taut physique as it was revealed piece by piece in the soft lamplight of the room.

"Rest assured I am here selfishly, Lady," The Prince said, naked at last. Already erect, his large phallus brushed against Eron's full, swaying breasts when he grasped her shoulders and leaned down to kiss her parted lips. "The Harbormaster is trusted to secrecy in this building, which is why my father met you here, I'm sure." He pulled Eron up off of the bed and encircled her with muscled arms, kissing her soft neck. "However, if he has a peephole or a necromancer with which to spy upon this room," he shrugged lightly, "this I do not know."

Eronica playfully hit him and then surrendered to his embrace. "He'd better not."

"Indeed."

"This changes nothing," she assured him with a note of harshness, though neither of them was listening. "I've wanted you, I admit. But I'll not be your concubine when I return."

"Lovers I can live with," he grunted, attacking her chest and swollen peaks with his thick tongue. When he kissed her again, it was a claiming of her body, despite Eron's warnings. She could not help but express her capitulation with a sigh.

Corine writhed in her bonds on the cooling bed and whimpered slightly.

Henrick stopped his ministrations and rested his forehead against Eron's. "I think someone feels left out," she whispered.

"Indeed."

Henrick took Eron's hand and led her back to the bed. "Turn around," he told her, facing her to the foot of the bed. Eron took the lead and got down on all fours over her mewing friend, spreading the girl's legs and lowering herself to dine on Corine's sweet juices. She dropped her own hips, teasing Corine's face as she thrust her ass high so that the prince could take her. Henrick too straddled Corine's head while he worked his engorged cock into the tight confines of Eron's quim. She moaned and settled her backside towards him, impaling herself on his desire. Henrick wasn't the largest she'd ever been with, but he was certainly on the list, and his strength and vitality were worth the wait. She dropped her head again, letting the long, dark waves of her hair rest on Corine's thighs. Eron looked between their bodies briefly, watching through the shadows as the Prince's speared his member into her inch by agonizing inch while his full balls brushed the nose and questing tongue of Corine. Hungrily the servant lapped at the flesh of both as their thrusting action began in earnest.

Eronica licked and sucked at Corine's slit, then dove deeper. She could feel the girl quiver beneath them, though if it was from her attentions or from the excitement of a threesome with the most powerful young man in the realm, Eron did not know.

Henrick's hands on her hips and the pumping quickness of his fucking would have been enough to quickly drive Eron to her first orgasm, but the darting tongue that worked feverishly to pleasure both her own clit and the hot skin slapping her backside crashed the wave over her faster than she might have guessed. Eron bit Corine's thigh to keep from screaming. "Gods, harder," she begged hoarsely, and met the Prince's thrusts eagerly.

Henrick complied, working a wet thumb into her tight anus with deliberate slowness while his driving cock began slamming her harder and faster. Eron stabbed at the hardened nub of Corine's pussy with her own hot mouth and teeth while pumping at the soaked girl with two fingers, trying to send her over the edge before her own second orgasm could claim her. The scene was obviously enough to hasten the Prince towards his own tolerance. "Gods," he groaned, pulling free long enough to let Corine lick the shaft before he stabbed back into her Lady.

It was all Eron could take. She screamed against her friend's quivering mound, collapsing her chest atop the heaving abdomen of the serving girl while her climax overtook her. Still she tried desperately to make her friend cum as well, forcing a third finger into her and quickening the pace despite her fatigue. Henrick pulled free and Eron could feel his heat along her bare back as he repositioned himself to dip his moist cock into Corine's waiting mouth. The girl suckled greedily at the offered member, taking him deep into her throat with ease. When Eron rubbed her thumb over the hardened clit again, Corine bucked and thrashed, exploding at last. She moaned her pleasure around the shaft in her mouth, then cried out when he pulled free. Henrick grasped himself by the hilt for a moment before squirting pearly cum onto Corine's face and Eron's backside. She could feel the hot, sticky fluid slide off of her backside, dripping back to land on Corine's waiting, panting tongue.

Eron rolled off of her friend and lay there catching her breath. It had been a long day, and the session had left her more spent than she cared to admit. The Prince, to his credit, dismounted easily, a testament to his vigor. He untied Corine's bonds, and she sat up quickly in his arms. Eron was glad that her servant resisted the urge to say anything meaningful or perhaps even tasteless, such as "My Prince." Instead she simply thanked His Majesty and then blushed, disentangling herself from his embrace. He kissed her lightly, then leaned over to Eron. "My Lady?"

"Your Majesty." She acknowledged. "You were right to stay."

"You don't have to just say that because of who I am," he offered.

"And you didn't have to possess us simply because of who you are," she told him. "In any case, your betrothed is a lucky woman."

Henrick III smiled at that. "Thank you."

"Thank you," Eron said with a kiss.

Corine sighed against the pillows. "Thank you," she sang to them, drunkenly waving one hand in the air at them.

"She's very cute," he whispered.

"Don't you dare," Eron admonished. "She's the only friend I have on this trip, and she's taken with you enough as it is."

"Indeed." He rose and grabbed his clothing, putting on his hose. "I've taken up enough of My Lady's time. And her servant's," he said with a wink to Corine. When he was finished dressing, he leaned over the nude form of Eron and whispered into her ear. Again she was struck with the fact that he might actually care. "Take heed, Lady. I know whatever task father sends you on is dangerous and steals you from our home for far too long. Be careful in your endeavor, for Capriana wants you both back safe and sound."

For a moment, Eron almost wanted to give in and stay. To live a simpler life by far and not go away on some adventure that put her in harm's way more times than she cared to guess. To simply become the Concubine of a Prince who was kind enough—at least as rich politicians went—and stay pampered and warm within the palace walls.

But that was not to be. She wanted for herself, and first she had a duty and a promise to perform. She couldn't be bothered with a foolhardy love for a Prince she could never be equal to, though it took much to push her emotions aside at that moment. "Thank you, Henrick." She kissed him deeply and looked him in the eyes. "We'll be careful, and we'll be back. Just don't let the King forget about us out there."

The Prince raised an eyebrow at that, but did not search for answers. He stood, patting Corine's hip playfully as he made to sneak back out. "Good night, ladies. Good Journey, and thanks for a fun evening." He left the room as silently as he had entered.

Corine sighed again. "Good night, My Prince."

Eron groaned and hit her servant with a pillow. "Go to sleep, wench. We've a long day tomorrow."

"Yes, Lady."

As Eron drifted off to welcome oblivion, her thoughts were soon troubled by images of dark men in billowing cloaks working hot, dirty hands over the frail flesh of slave girls sold to the highest bidder. Not for the first time did she wonder if she was up to this task.

Chapter 2

Capriana was no longer visible. The haze of the 'Sea of Blue Longing' and the curvature of the globe had seen to that. But Eron was long from safety, she knew, and darker waters lay ahead. The *Black Kettle* rolled over the spraying waves towards the lands to the south. The trip thus far had been uneventful and the crew kind enough to leave the ladies alone, though not without long glances from lustful eyes. The harbormaster must have paid the crew well indeed.

Eron wondered what cargo it was that the *Kettle*'s captain had been told he 'must' get through dangerous waters and 'safely to Morbindar's islands.' Then she realized that a detailed lie was one more doomed to fail. She was sure now that he had simply been given a box and a course and paid to ask no questions. In truth, they were delivering two women into the hands of Shebwai, whether privateers, pirates, or the Sultan's navy found them first. She didn't know whether to pity the seemingly kind crew for what might befall them, or shrug off the ignorant captain who had been paid to touch nothing, including the Lady and her servant. But this was war, and in all wars there were casualties.

"You'll get sunburn," Corine chided. "Come back under the sails, away from the railing."

Eron looked down at the exposed swells of her breasts, already turning pink. She'd kept herself and her servant mostly covered for much of the trip, as much not to attract the crew as simply not to advertise. Now, though, she felt safe enough to allow her natural charms a bit of showing in the lighter dresses she owned. Besides, if they were attacked, Eron wanted to make certain that whoever captured her knew exactly how much she would be worth in the Shebwai slave market.

From the corner of her eye she could see a barefoot crewman watching her from the rigging. Bored and frustrated, Eron fought the urge to tug childishly at the drawstrings of her cotton neckline and show off more to her voyeuristic watcher. Instead she placed her hands on her corset and drew in a breath. The sea air billowed her skirts around her ankles and her hair across her stinging lips. "Have you asked the captain how far we've come?" the impatient Lady asked.

Corine rolled her eyes. "For the third time, yes, and we're not near enough to anyplace we want to be, yet." She leaned in, adding under her breath, "We're not due to stray into enemy waters for days yet, Eron. You're going to pace a hole in the deck if you don't stop thinking about it."

In private, during their nights in the cabin together trying to make merry of their plight, Eron had whispered at last some of the plan to her friend. Fortunately it had not weakened Corine's resolve. Still, she dared not say more for fear of prying ears. "But I can think of little else," she admitted at last. "Next time I bring a book."

Corine looked at her from beneath long lashes, murmuring, "I'm sure I could help you think of other things."

"You're incorrigible," Eron gasped. "Is that all you think about?"

"It was what I was trained for, mistress," Corine shrugged. "And it's better than some alternatives." She took Eron's arm and steered her towards the doors leading below deck. "Come on. Let's get your mind off things."

The *Kettle*'s captain was on the wheel deck above the stairs. The middle-aged man eyed the girls with a slight smile of contempt. "Going below, ladies?"

"We're off to do some needlepoint," Corine offered, fanning herself. "'Tis too hot up here."

The captain and his mate eyed each other, sharing a private joke. "Aye," was all he said, and waved them away. Suddenly Eron didn't feel so bad about exposing these simpletons to whatever fate awaited them in the coming days.

The love play the women shared in the next hour was stifled and hot, with attempts to keep quiet being reduced to muffled cries into their pillows. They passed the time as need be, making certain no one could hear what they were doing and somehow feel 'invited' by it. Sweaty and spent, they both lay naked on the wet sheets, staring up at the ceiling as they tried to cool down.

"Maybe we shouldn't do this during daylight hours," Corine admitted. "Below decks is stagnant from the sun's heat above."

"I said as much," Eronica reproached. "Still, it's hardly worse than the sauna back at the *Chateau*."

"Gods," Corine exclaimed. "That was hell."

Eron thought back to the pain and pleasure of those days. "Yes, but it could also be rather heavenly." She took her friend's hand.

The *Chateau De Chaine*'s sauna had been huge; a stone and wood set of rooms kept constantly steamed. Depending on one's current level of expertise in whatever field she was being trained, girls had been brought into the bath chambers for different reasons and lengths of time. Women who wished to learn Dominance to better their sexual prowess or simply elevate their social position first had to learn to submit to a higher mistress and the very elements themselves. For this Eron had been chained within the sauna several times and treated to beatings or simply left bound and sweaty in the moist heat. On the other hand, women learning to be submissive—to be more sexually desirable by Lords, Ladies, Housemasters or Royalty—had been brought to the sauna for lengthy sessions of varying bondage and domination, often ending in forced orgasm and then a lengthy stay in the steam, still bound. It was here that Eron and Corine had met under the tutelage of Mistress Chandrice, who had first blissfully tied the two girls together and yet later defined their positions as Lady and Servant to each other.

Of course, different mistresses had brought the girls to the steam chambers for their own reasons, as well. Eron and Corine had discovered this for themselves first hand when they had been caught sneaking in to one of the kitchens out of turn. Mistress Flagen had been the one to discover the girls, and she was keen to reduce girls to wailing, quivering masses left chained and unfulfilled in the sauna for hours after she was finished with them. She was cruel, but Flagen knew how to heighten pleasure and endurance, and taught the lash as both a caress or as something harsher.

Eron shivered slightly and broke her reverie, going to the cabin's small chest-of-drawers to begin getting dressed. "Do you ever wish for Mistress Chandrice?"

"I suppose. She was very beautiful and kind—in her way." Corine looked away for a moment with a smile before steering the conversation into 'deeper' waters. "So, tell me; The Prince: What's he really like?"

Eronica groaned. "A one track mind, that's what you have, girl."

"*Grahrk, ho!*" came a voice from well above-deck. Instantly the boards above the girls' heads were rumbling with the sounds of rushing feet moving to and fro to posts and points of vantage. The crew was alarmed.

The two young women looked at each other with concern. "Was that the crow's nest?" Corine asked.

"Sounded like it," Eron answered. "What's a Grahrk?"

Corine had lived closer to port cities in her youth, and she was up instantly, throwing a shift over her head and grabbing a corset to secure it. "A beast of the sea. A serpent that can reach sizes to rival a whale."

"They sink ships?"

Corine shrugged, wide-eyed and worried. "If the tales of seafaring men are to be believed."

Eron was beginning to hate sea voyages.

The men were all aligned along one side of the ship, some standing against the banister, others climbing the rigging. All eyes were on the distant horizon. At first, Eron could see nothing.

"Where away?" Corine asked the closest deckhand.

Without taking his gaze from the far off stretch of ocean, the young crewman pointed to a spot near a patch of low clouds. "There," he said in an outlander's accent. "He's submerged at the moment, but he'll be back up."

Eron watched the spot the sailor had indicated. As she waited, she realized that the area was not ringed by clouds, but by a mist. It was as if a small, localized fog were trailing just that minute area. "What's that mist?"

"Could be anything," the same crewman answered. "A coming fogbank, a school of whales dancing."

"Don't be daft, man," another answered. "More likely a ship shrouded by spell than a natural mist."

The words of the older man caught Eron's attention for a moment. She found the idea of a shrouded ship shadowing them within visual distance as a disturbing possibility. Who could afford such spells but a navy, and for which country? Was a Kingdom fleet sailing these waters, or was the Shebwai navy finally stalking her vessel. Such heart-shuddering thoughts were again put aside as the crew exclaimed aloud, heralding the second appearance of the Grahrk.

"He's a big bastard. Could be as long as forty meters."

Eron's jaw dropped. The creature was still far off, but its thick coils were evident in the failing sunlight. It was like a giant snake of the sea, portions of it dipping in and out of the cresting waves. The colors were bands of crimson, black, and gold, made up evidently of shimmering scales and trailing hair or fins, Eron couldn't tell. The giant head with its open maw dove back into the depths, stealing their view of the beast once more. "Gods."

"Aye," the older crewman answered, turning away from the scene. "He's gone back to the deep. No use staring now."

Captain James Jovark of the *Angry Goddess* put his coat back on and trudged back up to his command deck. "At ease, men," he called to his crew. He gave a roguish grin to all within visibility and tied back his waves of long, dark hair, trying to act calm. "Stow those harpoons and secure for silent running. Mean Ben's done the work needed."

The crew laughed quietly and began to store the rest of the long harpoons along the ship's polished deck. The second mate had managed to hit and scare off the Grahrk with a single throw, but James wanted to make certain that it hadn't alerted the ship he was chasing to his position or colors. He snapped his fingers at Jack Kloot, holding out his palm to take the offered spyglass.

"The spell is unchanged," the stringy young magician claimed. "The Grahrk got close to us, but not so close that it doused our shroud," Jack said proudly.

"'The spell is unchanged, *captain*'," James corrected. "You spell-casting kids may hate authority figures that aren't magic-users, Jack, but remember that I keep you alive on this ship, regardless of your own abilities."

"Aye," Jack sighed, resigned.

James sighed. "'Aye, *sir*.'" Shaking his head, he took the charmed spyglass, the only item on the ship that could see through the mystical fog Jack Kloot had fashioned for them. Its lenses pierced the veil shrouding his giant vessel, peered across the vast waves and afforded James a clear view of his quarry, even as the last rays of the sun glinted across his tanned, handsome face. The wind pierced the vale of fog enough to ripple his silken, shirt. It felt good on his chest after so long, tracking their quarry from beneath the spell's strange shroud.

James's smile broadened and his sweeping view of the other ship's deck stopped, spying something that had not been there before. "Well, well," he said to himself as much as those around him. James stroked the rough goatee that framed his short beard, thinking of new possibilities. His eyes raked over the two female forms in their tightly bound gowns, each framed by halos of long hair. They stared back as though attempting to see him through the fog. The small redheaded one wore the collar of a servant, but she was young and pretty. The brunette, though, was a gorgeous specimen, with ample breasts and proud, beautiful features. Her dark eyes and lashes pierced his soul for a moment, and in that instant he wrongfully wondered if she could truly see him staring at her. The twitch in his breeches was enough to cast aside any momentary feelings of guilt. He was a pirate, after all. "Mister Bevisc," James called to the first mate.

"Aye, captain," Telorn Bevisc answered from the deck.

"Take the wheel. We go ahead as planned. We should overtake her before dawn."

"Aye, captain."

Eronica picked up a lantern and tapped her friend on the shoulder. "Let's turn in," she said.

"All right," Corine agreed, hiking up her skirts and turning away from the inky blackness of the night. There were no moons tonight, therefore no view of the sea as on other evenings. The air had become almost as still as the breaths of the crew. They were waiting quietly, each worried but silent. They all knew that a ship was out there in that fog, but whether it had moved off or was giving chase, no one dared jinx. The *Black Kettle* was not in Shebwai waters, as far as anyone knew, but they were close enough to make things uncomfortable for all aboard.

Eron closed the door to their cabin and motioned for her servant to be quiet. "We sleep," she whispered, "but do it dressed. We may have visitors tonight, and I'd rather feel a bit prepared for it."

Corine nodded, but she was scared. "Do you really think we'll be attacked tonight, Lady?"

Eronica did not answer.

She blew out the wick and tried to sleep.

Eronica started awake, swearing that the sound of an explosion had rattled her instantly into consciousness. Bellowed orders and loud commands from the deck above made Eron sit up and swing her legs off of the bed. She peered through the darkness at Corine when she began to stir.

"Mistress?"

"Corine," Eron breathed, sounding more excited than panicked. "I think we're under attack!" The sound of canon fire from nearby confirmed Eron's suspicions. Her breath caught in her throat when the shuffle of feet and screams of the injured or dying began to bring the cold reality of the situation to Eron. "Wait here."

"My Lady, don't!"

But Eron was already out of their small cabin and rushing up the hall and stairs to the deck. She swung wide the door in unthinking haste and gasped, finding a grueling scene being played out before her wide eyes.

A second ship, huge even in the dim light of torches along the decks, was coming alongside the *Kettle*. The galleon had emerged from the mystical fog that had veiled the craft until closing within near boarding range. The few deck canons the smaller merchant vessel was equipped with for defense were all glowing a curious orange, as though turning back into molten steel in front of their helpless operators. Eron knew that some sort of spell had been placed on the guns making a boarding party's coming an easy task. Crewmen stood at the ready with pistols and swords in hand, and some fired muskets across the water at unseen foes in the dark. The answering rifles silenced many of the *Kettle*'s men before they could fire again. One round smashed into the wooden doorframe above Eron's head and she shrieked, ducking as she closed the door enough to watch through the cracks.

The growling sneers of the enemy could be heard loudly now, gaining Eron's attention. A cold chill of fear gripped her heart as she at last spied the attackers standing on the railing of the galleon with blades in hand.

Pirates!

"My Gods," Eron whispered. "What have I done?" She had no way of knowing whether or not these scoundrels even worked in any capacity for the Sultan of Shebwai. Now the *Kettle*'s crew hadn't a chance. She and Corine were sure to be captured or killed.

She could only hope that the latter would not be the case.

Eron continued to watch through the partially opened door as the battle was joined on the deck. Sailors from the attacking vessel had swung over on ropes and drew their swords and pistols, attacking the crew. Eron watched in shock as the captain quickly fell, her hand flying to her lips to check a scream before it could escape at the sight of a shot piercing his barreled chest. The aging seafarer fell to the deck with a sickening thud. She then saw the first mate—a man she had barely known, much less respected or cared for—leap onto the deck from the command platform. His cocked pistol took the nearest pirate in the face, and his curved sword slashed another pair before they could move to intercept. Suddenly the mate—this figure of typical manly bravado and stupidity in Eron's eyes—was transformed into a gallant fighter who would defend his crew unto death.

The *Kettle*'s first mate fought his way through the marauders, reinvigorating his crewmates and spurring them back into action. The defense surged forward despite being outnumbered by the pirates, but the hope was only brief.

A silhouette swung through the night, emerging from the smoke and mists and landing upon the deck. This new figure of a man had waited, unseen in the shadows of his own galleon until now, but the moment his boots touched the *Kettle's* deck Eron was struck by his presence. Tall and powerfully built, the man was shrouded still in black sashes and leather belts lashing a forest-green frock coat. Dark ringlets of long hair fell in waves from beneath a large black hat. A wide grin split a goatee streaked with scarlet and he drew a wicked looking rapier from the scabbard hanging from his baldric. The Galleon's captain bellowed a roar of challenge at his foe.

The *Kettle's* mate turned just in time to parry the first blow, countering with a strong set of slashes meant to sever the pirate captain's arms. The captain's thin but lightning-quick rapier easily held the mate off, then stabbed at him in fast, successive strikes that finally found their mark. The mate reeled, his heavier blade dashed away by the sleek rapier.

"Surrender," the pirate captain ordered him at sword point.

The mate took one step back, as though astonished that he had lost the spectacular duel. "Never," he answered.

A moment later a crimson stain streamed down the mate's shirt from where he had been stabbed. His legs failed him, and he collapsed to the deck.

The Lady Eronica didn't know how to feel. She had never seen true battle, and never really faced death—not like this. It was sickening and shocking and terrible. Somehow this figure, with his chiseled looks, though covered in soot and sweat, had made the spectacle almost... exciting. Eron's breath caught in her throat when she thought the tall captain had spotted her hiding place and would come next for *her*. But the captain turned away, and once more she was left wondering just how to feel.

Eron did not have long to contemplate the matter; a new figure stepped from the mist and paused when he looked her direction. Moving away from the battle and towards her hiding place, this man was staring right at her.

He was younger and less physically developed. Simple robes and a long leather belt seemed baggy on his lean frame, but his eyes held an eerie power that stopped Eron from fleeing. Before the youth had even reached the door it swung open, seemingly of its own accord. Eron gasped in shock as the possessed door revealed her hiding place. Whatever hold the young magician had on her broke in that instant, and she turned to run. She made it down two steps when a blue light enveloped her, numbing her limbs. Eron looked back over her shoulder to gaze in awe at the powers of the young man, but the blue haze was even more intense in his eyes, and she was drawn into his vision. The flash that filled Eron's mind was enough to knock her unconscious.

James checked to see if any of his men were looking. When he saw that all were too occupied with moving the booty back onto the galleon or tending wounds, he dropped his smile and regarded the blood on his hands. He'd hated to become so personally involved, but enough of his boys had died for one day. He'd had to swing aboard the merchant vessel and kill the man spurring the defenders back into the fray, but he'd hated to do it.

James's men were bastards all. It had been less than two years since they had all been reduced to murdering cutthroats in order to save their own hides, but he would honor that decision and keep them breathing as long as he could. James preferred to dirty his own hands as little as possible, leaving the necessary killing to his crew, but a captain had to do whatever it took to keep them all sailing another day. He wiped the blood away as best he could manage on a strip of cloth, finding a clean spot to do the same with his sword.

"Where you want 'em, cap'n?" Billy and the magician Jack Kloot were hauling the unconscious redhead across the gangplank and onto the deck of his *Angry Goddess.*

James ignored the drying smears still coated to his fingers and shot a knowing grin at the men. "I've not yet decided what immediate fate should befall the serving girl," he said, then thrust his chin at the brunette about to be carried over as well. "That one stays in my cabin this night."

There was a laugh from members of the crew close enough to hear the command. "I'll make sure she's properly stowed, J.J.," Telorn Bevisc said as he helped haul the stunned cargo aboard.

James nodded in thanks, patting his first mate on the shoulder. "Good man."

"Like hell," Telorn laughed.

"Like hell any of us are," Billy quipped. "Eh, Ben?"

Mean Ben only had a slurred response, but it was a decidedly vulgar one.

James turned back to the scene at hand, watching as the sea began to claim the burning *Kettle*. He shook his head only briefly, hoping his expression revealed nothing of the small but not insignificant grief he felt over the matter. He pushed such futile ideas aside and remembered to concentrate on the matter at hand. Such thoughts made life unbearable, and times for he and his crew were tough enough. Capriana's deceit had made certain of that two years hence. Now he just wanted to keep his lads as happy as possible for however much longer those cheating Gods above allowed.

James glanced again at the brunette being taken past him to his quarters. She was beautiful, even in sleep. Her fashion-conscious and richly tailored gowns marked her as a Lady of Capriana, probably of some standing and therefore of little care. She would fetch a high price on the Shebwai market for certain, but first he would exact a little revenge against her homeland by way of her flesh. Such things were all that remained to brighten his days.

The redhead was a boon, though. It had been a few months since any attractive women had been captured, and seeing as James was taking the brunette for at least the night, he would probably have to give the servant to the crew. He was uncertain he wished to leave one woman—even a Capriana serving wench—to the crew alone after such a dry spell, but he didn't know if he had any other choice at this point. James shrugged, wondering if the matter was even up to him. He could leave such worries to Telorn if nothing else.

The *Black Kettle* gave one last deathly sigh as it sank beneath the waves, gone forever with her brave—if stupid—crew. Captain James Jovark of the Grey Isles surveyed his battle-hardened ship and its own group of parasites and wondered who the luckier group was. Reminding himself of his initial decision two years back that life as slaves was still life on the seas at least, he spit over the side of the *Goddess* at his vanquished foes. His life was better, by Gods. If it meant drowning himself in the few pleasures he could find anymore to prove that to himself each day, then he would.

"Mister Ben!"

Mean Ben, the ship's second mate, had finished securing the serving girl's bonds behind her back, though his hands were still roaming over the unconscious girl's curves. Grudgingly the filthy sailor tore his blood-shot eyes off of her to regard his captain. "Aye, cap'n?"

"Fetch the First Mate."

Ben looked down at the girl again.

"Now, Ben."

"Aye." Ben disappeared into the ship's cabins. When he returned with Telorn, James waved the grimy second mate into the rigging.

"J.J.?" Telorn wondered quietly.

James faked a wide grin. "Break out the ale, and be quick about it. There's drinking to be done, mate."

Telorn smiled genuinely and cocked his head toward the girl laying face down on the deck. "And that one?"

James feigned an expression and half-shrugged. "I leave her fate in your charge. I'll be too drunk to care, I can promise you that. All I can say is she's worth good money in Shebwai, so keep her intact."

Telorn's demeanor changed slightly, but he whispered, "Shebwai keeps more than half of the money owed us, much less what we catch. Maybe we should keep the girl for our own just to stick it to them. We could leave her in some port..."

"I won't have it," James quipped, anxious to have a mug in his hand. "We agreed that this was how it was to be, so let's make the most of it and get on with our lives." He pointed at the redhead. "No permanent marks, and that means watch Ben around her. Now off with you; one keg for the night and some salted beef for all."

Telorn pushed his spiteful idea aside easily and nodded. "Aye cap'n." He turned to the closest sailor, Billy, who grinned at the task they were set upon. "Help me take the girl below to the hold *after* we bring the keg up. How much ale and beef have we?"

"Plenty," the sailor said, "given what we brought aboard just now."

"Drinks for all!" James exclaimed, rousing a cheer from the crew.

He soon found himself with his desired mug in his hand and a satisfactory feeling of inebriation sloshing through his brain. The drink helped force his thoughts away from the death of the day and onto the waiting girl. Long auburn curls and a full chest swayed in front of him as though he could see her dancing. She was beautiful; he was sure of that much regardless of how briefly he had seen her thus far. Her breeding promised fleshly pleasures that his own aching need called out to. But she was from Capriana, and that fact demanded retribution.

Yes, he thought, *I'll make her mine several times over before I hand her over to any landlubbing Shebwai son of a bitch.*

Chapter 3

Eronica stirred, waking slowly from a deep dream. She could still feel the movement of a ship beneath her, but the sounds above had changed. Her ears could discern the resonant metallic clicking of a mantle clock in the room and she could smell expensive woods reminding her of crafted furniture back home.

Her groggy mind tried to ascertain her bearings, but she quickly found her range of movements limited in the extreme and fear began to unsettle her stomach. Eron's arms and legs were bound; ropes at her wrists and ankles made it impossible to escape from the plush bed she realized she'd been constrained to.

Whatever spell had put her to sleep was making it hard to concentrate, though she tried to take stock through her confusion. She was tied down, apparently in the cabin of a sailing vessel, undoubtedly that of the captain that had attacked her ship…

Pirates!

Now she remembered; the attack on her ship that obviously had made her a prisoner and sent much of the *Kettle*'s crew to their deaths. But where was Corine? A terrible doubt that anyone beside herself had survived made Eron momentarily lapse into despair. She lay spread-eagle and gagged to a large wooden bed, at the mercy of a pirate crew, her dress the only defense against whom-ever came through that door. She swallowed the tears that threatened to well her eyes.

Taking deep breaths to help calm herself, Eron tried to focus her eyes on the room she had been left in. The bedposts her wrists were tethered to were exquisitely carved, though the style suggested that the Grey Isles were most likely their artist's country of origin. The clock she could hear was on a fine dresser near a large stained-glass window, presumably adorning the rear of the ship. This was definitely the galleon that had attacked the *Kettle*. Above the double-doors was inscribed the words *Angry Goddess*. The name struck Eron in much the same way the appearance of the dark rogue who piloted the vessel had the night before. He would be coming for her, she thought, and with that her breathing had to be consciously slowed once more. For all she knew she was now a slave on a vessel with no intention of taking her to Shebwai waters, much less home.

Muffled laughter met her ears from somewhere outside of cabin's thick walls. "*Trapped*," her slurred mind exclaimed. "*This is not the* Chateau, *Eron. Here you are truly alone and at the mercy of others. Gods, what were you thinking?*"

Eron's dark curls were splayed about her immobilized arms forming a halo around her face. She tried to look down to see the state of her clothes and body: The low-cut dress seemed sooty from the attack on her torched vessel—or from the filthy hands that had borne her from it's deck—but otherwise the garment was undamaged. She could still feel the stockings on her legs, and the small knife kept in the garter at her inner thigh. Eron had secreted it there before turning in the previous evening. Deciding that she seemed relatively unmolested during the time of her unconsciousness, Eron knew the probability of lay immediately ahead, and it did nothing to calm her nerves.

Pulling against the ropes that had wrenched her wrists above her head, Eron found little slack and tight bonds. The gag was relatively loose but held by a well-tied ribbon. Her trepidation increased when she heard voices nearing the cabin door. Deep, dark voices that spoke heartily of things she could not quite make out. There were laughs, and large boot-steps, some leading away, but one set headed straight for the room the Lady Eronica now occupied alone.

"*Trapped*," she thought again. "*You must calm yourself, girl, if you hope to survive through to Shebwai and beyond.*" But calm did not come. Instead her breathing became shallow, and the pounding in her chest drowned out the ticking of the mantle clock.

Soon the door opened, and through the haze in her mind she watched a man of rugged good looks and long dark hair walk in. This time Eron could not control her breathy moans at the site of her oppressor; the same man whom she had watched swing onto the deck of the *Kettle* and duel its

First Mate to the death. He was smiling as he looked down at her, and she knew her own fearful eyes betrayed her.

His clothes were of fine weave, but dirty from long use on the sea. The slender rapier hung at his hip from a black leather baldric. Long belts and sashes cinched his waist, and his shirtfront was open, revealing a muscular chest and curls. In his hand he held a mug of wine, its contents spilling slightly over the rim and dribbling over ringed fingers when he erratically turned to close the door. He was drunkenly raking his brown eyes over her body, drinking in every curve through the folds of her dress, and it only made Eron and her still-recovering mind all the more alarmed.

She had to turn this to her advantage somehow, she knew. The rogue was not uncomely. His wind-swept, suntanned looks would have been a welcome change at court, had his clothes simply been cleaner and his demeanor somehow improved. Indeed, he was every bit as well built and frighteningly real as Eron had feared from the first moment she had laid eyes on him. But the man's handsome features were belied by the rakish sneer of his intent. His gaze brought both fear and heat to the very core of her soul. *"How could any adversary win in the face of such self-satisfaction?"* Eron thought. She now understood why the *Kettle*'s mate had been defeated, though for ultimately different reasons.

"Good evening, My Lady," he said at last, setting down his mug. "I am Captain Jovark. I see my men have had the good sense to restrain you properly to my bed. I trust you will not mind if I take advantage of that good sense."

Eron tried to yell a hastily formed obscenity at him, but found it choked pathetically back by the gag. She watched as he knelt on the bed, dropping his sword and belts to the floor. His hand reached for her bound ankle. In vain she tried to pull at the ropes, twisting away from his touch as desperation began to sweep over her mind. It only seemed to spur him on as he watched her wiggle on his mattress.

"My Lady is not pleased with my company? How terrible for you, since I am about to do whatever I wish to you," taunted Jovark. His hand ran up Eron's stocking to her knee, dragging the expensive dress along with it. She held her breath, unable to meet his gaze and somehow captured by the site of him beginning to test her resolve. "And unless you want first your friend and then yourself to entertain the entire crew tonight, I suggest you learn how to enjoy it."

Eron breathed a moment's sigh of relief. Corine was alive. That was at least one question answered. She ignored his threat and looked away in defiance.

Jovark rolled his eyes. "Very well," he said, reaching down beside the bed where his belts lay. Eron didn't bother to look at whatever item he'd produced until it struck her. The leather flogger slapped her cleavage and resounded along the portions of her corset that its tawny straps fell upon. Stunned, Eron glared at the smug captain. He looked back as if to say *'I told you so,'* then set the flogger down next within his reach.

She watched him, feeling in retrospect like a startled deer. Eron's eyes rested on the captain's muscular chest as he revealed it. She was unable to match his stare yet unwilling to study him groping her, so she was left contemplating the hair upon his breast or the ceiling beyond.

Jovark knelt over her exposed stocking-clad calf, and his expression made it obvious how he felt about the clean lines and grace of her stretched limb. His own dark curls fell about his face when he bent over to allow his lips to follow his fingers to her thigh. Eron gave an involuntary moan of fear through her gag. Damn whatever spell had been placed over her mind like a veil! She would make that young magician pay if she ever got the chance.

Momentarily the man's gruff fingers left her flesh, and Eron exhaled a brief respite. But Jovark ran a hand up over her dress to her heaving bust line, saying, "You are now my property, m'lady." Those dirty, bloodstained hands were roaming over her chest, though the stitches of Eron's gown held out against him. "At least until I sell you to the Sultan."

The Sultan! Than at least she was headed in the right direction. Now if Eron could only collect her wits long enough to survive the tribulations of this man's bed. She tried to remember something—anything—of what she had learned at the Chateau. Anything that would help her overcome what was happening to her. But Jovark's hands were nearly as hot as his breath, and his body was a threatening weight over her own helpless form. She managed only a whimper through the gag as her limbs pulled uselessly at their bonds.

Her dress hem was again rising up each leg inch by inch. "You *were* aware," the pirate captain slurred, "that the Sultan of Shebwai had employed many of the former kingdom pirates to help decimate the navy of your traitorous nation, did you not?" He was droning on, his voice thick with a need to drum fear into her being and make her body tremble beneath him. "Well, in your case it was a merchant vessel, not naval, but it matters not. What matters," he said, moving his face lower, "is that you are mine to do with as I please. And as you're the one tied down," he laughed, letting the thought trail off. For the briefest second, he ran the tip of his tongue around the exposed top of her right stocking. Eron's flesh shrank away from the questing organ, but her mind luxuriated at the feel of its surface on her skin. Then—suddenly—he was there, looking directly into her eyes with his warm, wine-laden breath on her face. "There's not a damned thing you can do about it, *My Lady*." Eron sobbed once, her breath catching in one last attempt to stare back defiantly. But he was already gone, his hands on her hips, his lips leaving a trail of kisses and tiny bites wherever his fingers clawed at her exposed cleavage.

He moved down. Eron could feel Jovark's breathing against both exposed thighs as her gown's many layers were gathered up past her stocking tops. She concentrated on her days at the *Chateau* again, and for the next few moments her mind trailed to days of pleasure.

His rough hands began running up her inner thighs—and then she remembered!

"Well," said Jovark, fingering the blade that rested alongside such soft, tender flesh. "My Lady is a minx with claws, I see. How naughty of a proper young woman so beautiful, learned, and curvaceous as yourself to carry so lethal a weapon in such a…secret place." He laughed and pulled the knife ever so slowly from between her tingling skin and the garter at her left thigh. As he did so, Jovark deliberately allowed his knuckles to brush higher, sending a wave of shivering temptation up through the center of Eron's body. The blade came away with anguishing tease, and the following stillness made her fear this man even more. Jovark leaned on one elbow, looking Eron in the eyes while holding the blade in his large fingers. When he smiled, it was not a mirthful thing, and he removed his shirt, adding to the threatening gesture. "I shall have to show My Lady what such a weapon is truly useful for."

With astonishing speed and agility he slashed upward, cutting the ribbons that bound the front of Eron's dress. She gasped at the ferocity of the action and the intentions it predicted, turning her breathing into brief, ragged gasps. Eron could only gape down helplessly at the exposing of her own body as he tore open the corset with his bare hands and pulled the front of her shift down to expose her breasts.

"Damn," he said appreciatively at the sight.

The pirate grunted as he made short work of her garments, grinning wickedly as he revealed more and more of her stunning body to his scrutinizing view. He produced her knife again, using it to slice her corset away at the shoulders and shred the gown from the waist down. Jovark then stabbed the blade into the wooden frame just beyond Eron's reach, but before she even had time to react to the shocking gesture he'd used his bare hands to finish tearing her shift in half. In moments Eron realized that she was naked from her neck to her stockings.

Left gasping and writhing in her bonds, Eron only turn her head away as his face dove at her, succeeding in leaving her neck and earlobe open to attack. Eron arched, trying desperately to push his hot body off of her own, but it simply opened her senses further to the feel of his chest hairs rubbing against the milky swells of her breasts. He grasped one with his left hand, groaning approval at the fullness. Her nipples traitorously hardened to a painful state when his teeth claimed the edge of her ear, signing due claim to her flesh. A wetness began to collect between Eron's legs.

"A Lady of Capriana," he mused teasingly into her ear. The close sensation made the hair on the back of Eron's neck rise. "Probably schooled at one of those chateaus. You should be enjoying this, then." Jovark's hand worked around from thigh and over hip. Moving down, it palmed the down-covered mound of her cleft, and Jovark's fingers began to quest. "Are you?" She bucked and thrashed, vainly attempting to deny the digits entry, but as one and then a second found their mark, she knew that they slid easily into her slick channel. Jovark grunted a mocking laugh at this new victory. "I'll take that as a 'yes'."

Eron tried to scream her protest at him, but instead her head was swimming with conflict, allowing only a groan to escape her lips. What was wrong with her? This murderer was going to rape her, and while she had anticipated such possibilities upon taking this assignment, it was something she should have been able to detach herself from if needed. She had intended to seduce her captors when required, play them for fools at all times, and deflect them whenever she decided necessary. Instead she had been reduced to a snared rabbit staring into the eyes of a wolf and betrayed by a body that ached to be used. She blushed with shame when Jovark pulled his fingers free and she knew they were covered with her own want.

His smile broadened as he sat back, straddling her hips. "My magician's spells may help fuel your desire," he said, studying the moisture on his fingertips. "But whether you were trained to lay with men while bound or not, you *like* it."

Eron couldn't deny it, though she now chalked up a second reason to kill that magician pirate if ever she had the chance. Instead the helpless young Lady started to shake her head at her assailant, hoping somehow to put him off, convince him he was a stupid, wholly-incorrect lying bastard. Rather she fell further victim to her body's own desires, going queasy at her center when she watched him lick his offending fingers clean of her scent.

Eron was shamefully reminded of the dreams she'd had of the Sultan when she was a girl; the late night fantasies of being in the harem and made love to in decadent ways against her will in a land of beauty. Of being spanked and tied and used as she had heard they treated their slaves. As she aged the fantasies had become dreamy escapes from her routine of being in control, but not desires she truly felt she wanted fulfilled at the loss of all power. She could only guess what was in store for her now at the hands of this rogue as he spoke to her. Regardless of the fear and panic of her completely hopeless situation—and perhaps because of it—the truth was that she was shivering in anticipation.

"You are a strikingly beautiful young woman," he assessed proudly, and the words struck Eron back to the moment. Jovark leaned over her again and began squeezing her large breasts, cruelly running both fingertips and mouth over the soft pink skin. His lips were like brands, feeling somehow larger and more forceful than they had looked. He ran a trail of saliva from one swollen mound to the other as he laved them with his rough tongue, tickling her ribs with his reddened beard. Eron whimpered a protest against the sensuous attack and trembled despite her rigid stance.

"Mine," was his simple claim, and his hand found the moist center between Eron's undefended thighs. His tongue traced circles of molten steel across her flat belly, belying the rough effrontery of the two fingers now sliding in and out of her. She tried to suck her stomach in as though she could avoid his ministrations, but the movement only impaled her pussy further onto his digits. Jovark evidently took the motion as her want, and started delving deeper and harder into her, all the while rubbing at her hardening clit with his thumb. His free hand held Eron's right breast, kneading the swollen flesh and pinching the plump, stiff nipple, sending waves of unwanted pleasure to her core.

Damn this man and his resources! Eron had been left a panting harlot in his molding hands as though she were an inexperienced youth being tested on the *Chateau*'s devices once more. Only now she was a woman who knew the pleasures of the flesh and the retorts she was being denied. She wanted to scratch at him, kick him off of her and walk proudly away to show him what he could not have. Instead he was having her now, freeing his swollen manhood from his breeches with an available hand while the other pumped her closer and closer to a forced orgasm. It made her want him in a way she hated, but could not deny. Her body had been awakened to a terrible point of uncontrollable desire, and her panting gasps, droopy eyes and squirming body communicated this to her attacker in spades.

In one final act of disobedience, she bit the gag still holding her insults back. Baring her teeth, Eron narrowed her dark, tear-welling eyes at him and glared, but it was useless; her undulating hips ground down on his hand and rocked towards his nearly-freed cock in open want. Jovark vehemently grasped the knife above her and used it to cut the gag away, denying Eron even that defense.

As his hand spread her seeping womanhood's lips further and roughly molested her clit, he leaned down to mash his lips upon hers, diving into a kiss that she could only open herself to. Eron's breath came in raspy, wanton groans as their tongues battled for the supremacy of her mouth. Jovark triumphed yet again, sealing his open lips over hers and delving his tongue deep into its recesses. She accepted the defeat, sliding her tongue over his as it tangled her up and carried her away with its ferocity and taste. Even as she resigned herself to the moment's fate with acceptance of the only thing that could now quench her thirst, tears streamed from Eron's eyes as she squeezed them shut against what she new was coming.

Jovark was breathing hard into her ear again as he squeezed her breasts with his rough hand. "Oh, girl, but you do bewitch a man. I must have you. I've wanted to have you since the moment I spied you though the fog yesterday." His teeth and lips pulled at her rock-hard nipples as his fingers fumbled with her flesh, and for the briefest instant Eron wondered who was the more tortured. "And I will have you, body and soul. I demand it." Jovark's kiss and hands left her trembling body long enough to finish undressing himself. He stared at her as a hungry wolf about to gorge when he tore the leggings away and exposed himself completely.

Eron had but a moment to study the huge phallus the pirate captain sported before he was going to impale her upon it. She met his gaze, trying not to stare at the spear jutting towards her. Instead she seethed through ground teeth and tensed resolutely, screaming obscenities at him with only her eyes.

The shaft was long and thick, larger than most of the men Eron had been with, and certainly fuller in girth than any she had experienced. The head, pulsing and discolored with greedy imbibe, glistened slightly with a drop of pre-cum, and veins stood up along the rigid length. Though her lips were free and her mind fluent, no words of denial or slur escaped Eron's mouth. Reticent, she was ready for him to have her, though Eron did her best to look prepared to tear at his flesh with her teeth if necessary. She shook the sweat from her eyes.

He fell back upon her spread-eagle form, and Eron could feel his erection against her inner thigh, ready to take her with but the slightest forward movement. She wanted to curse him, to scratch him and then command him to fuck her—to make her his own and get it over with. Her body disagreed with her mind, hoping to the gods that he would fill her inch by languorous inch and slowly drag the oncoming climax from her shuddering form. She got both when Jovark settled his hips between her bound-apart thighs and thrust himself into her to the hilt. Eron screamed a hoarse peal of desire and pain that she was certain the whole ship could have heard. She blushed deeply as the scream became a drawn-out groan of pleasure as Jovark pulled slowly free, then slid back into her convulsing pussy. Her mind thought of Corine possibly hearing her being taken and of the crew that knew their captain was having his way with her.

"No," she said. But her body was a monster unto its own, and it longed to wrap itself around the man expertly fucking her. She no longer noticed the raw skin of her wrists still pulling at the ropes; just the never-ceasing waves of pleasure this blaggard seemed determined to torture her with.

He pulled free, then entered again, licking at her erect nipples, sucking at her neck, running hands over hips and thighs. He took her mouth again to sear them with kisses that she could no longer fight or deny, crushing away her protesting whimpers. She turned her face into the plush pillows surrounding her, gasping "No" once more, only to then moan and raise her hips to meet his thrusts.

Jovark growled in triumph.

Still inside of her, he leaned back and used the knife to quickly slice away the ropes that bound her ankles. He grabbed each with his fists and held her legs apart as he kneeled, driving his manhood into her, her feet still dangling the knotted bonds. She watched him study the form of her legs, thighs still clad in white stockings. She could do nothing but look up at him with her arms still tied high above her head, sweat dripping from every pore of exposed skin, her mouth hanging open in what she knew had to be wanton desire and not the defiance she tried to still project. Jovark wrapped her ankles around his back, then leaned forward and buried every thick inch of himself into Eron, eliciting a groan from her. Within moments her first orgasm crashed over her and she screamed again, twisting beneath his assault and calling out to the gods.

"Please! Oh, please, Gods," she cried, but even she no longer knew what it was she was asking of her deities.

Eron was on fire. She wrapped her limbs about his muscular body. She moaned again as his thrusts came faster and faster, again and again. He attacked her with animal intensity, hands and lips and tongue and thrusts of engorged cock threatened to send her flesh and soul over an edge into oblivion. But still she cried out in pleasure, her moans becoming gasps in time to each quick, hard pump into her. He grasped both nipples between his cruelly pinching fingers and did not let go, and she willed that he never would. It felt like time stood still; that the ravishing of her body would never end, and Eron was not sure she wanted it to. This moment could be the death of her for all she cared now. The pumping came quicker still as even Jovark made sounds of satisfaction mounting. Eron could perhaps have somehow kicked him off, now that her legs at least were free, but she could not have escaped on any account. She was pinned beneath this man, adrift on an open sea and ridden to the next plain.

Jovark bit her raw nipples and savaged her mouth again. Eron could do nothing but breathe into him with tiny sounds of longing. The spring winding within her was nearing its apex, and the engorging cock filling Eron told her that Jovark was also ready to explode. The walls of her womanhood clutched at him involuntarily, drawing him deep within herself as the captain's own grunts became more vocal. Jovark thread his fingers in her hair, forcing her to face him as he rode her to the breaking point. He licked her chin and lips before thrusting her head against his chest once his plunging hips became more demanding. Eron's body was awash in sweat, her hair plastered around her face and shoulders, and the sound of their skin meeting became a hurried slapping of wetness.

Jovark began to moan into her hair, supporting himself above her with both arms as he drove himself into Eron with finishing, decisive blows of glory. She felt him expand within her as he cried out with a great final roar. His shaft spiked home as he came, his seed spilling forth in gratifying climax that Eron's body echoed, and she nearly passed out in their shared exhaustion. At last Jovark fell spent upon her heaving breasts. She could only lie there with him still hard inside of her, with her arms limp in their bonds above her. She was completely and utterly ravished.

Eron began to drift off to sleep while the warmth that had spread over her body lingered still. Jovark's arm lay sprawled over her, cupping her breast. The cool sea air from the windows around them wafted over her damp, naked skin. Eron's hair stuck in sweaty ringlets to her face and neck. Her stockings were soaked through and her thighs felt bruised, her entire body depleted and yet satisfied. All these lingering feelings were still not enough to drive away the chafing ropes at her wrists, the shame on her red cheeks, or the thoughts of hopeless escape that threatened to coax her from sleep. But the exhaustion of the day—however she may have now regarded its events—soon claimed her as its own.

Chapter 4

Eron could hear the sounds of belts being buckled as the waves passed by the stern of the *Goddess*. The room was bright and the morning assailed her senses in unfair ways. She tried to stir, but found her wrists yet bound above her. She was thankful for the open windows, for despite her nakedness upon the strewn bedcovers the room was warm and bordering on stuffy. It would be a hot day.

"My Lady awakes," said captain Jovark. He glanced over at her as he finished adjusting his clothes. His smug smile roused conflicting emotions instantly within Eron as thoughts of the previous night returned. Anger quickly won her over, but she did not turn from his caressing glances.

Again Eron thought that he was very handsome, but cruel and uncaring, and she felt determined to make him understand that. "I am not your Lady, I am your captive," she said.

Jovark had stopped. He stared at her now, hard and studying. "You wish to protest the gifts I bestowed on your body last night, Lady of Capriana?"

"You're a bastard," she said simply. "You took me against my will."

Jovark chuckled low. "You seemed willing enough." He leaned towards her ear. Eron turned away, but did cringe from his side. "Arching, wet and wanting, I took you, yes… but you did desire it."

"And how much of that was your magician's spells?" she shot at him.

Jovark laughed aloud this time. "There was no 'spell'." Eron turned, shocked. The captain shrugged a little. "There's a disorientation from being knocked out by Mr. Kloot's arts, I know." He looked her in the eyes, conquering her with a single gaze that she could not pry away. "But that's all. The rest was you—and I." He knelt on the bed and took her chin in one large hand. "You enjoyed our coupling, woman. Stop denying it. While your beauty drove me past the base need to simply use you and in turn make you…" he paused, looking away for the briefest second, "…want me." His tone changed again, this time to harshness, "I am nonetheless willing to force you as I desire, whether you accept that or not. I'll not have you denying me, one way or the other."

Silence filled the room as Jovark left the bed and went to his dresser, where he began accessorizing his accoutrements. Eron could only lie there and think. His comments on her beauty and his desires for more than just her body touched something within her, albeit briefly. If he wasn't lying and there had been no spell that truly drove her to enjoying what had transpired between them, then she simply didn't know what to think. He was still a pirate, and probably just as soon a liar as a rapist and murderer. Still, she could not deny what he had awakened within her.

And she might be able to turn that to her advantage while aboard.

Eron couldn't be too quick to admit anything to him, but she still had weapons at her disposal if she could simply be free of her bonds and able to wield her body. Jovark might just then bend to her will, and Eron would then be in a position to make certain that she and Corine were safer, at least until they reached Shebwai.

"Unless you enjoy the site of a woman soiling your sheets, I suggest you free me," Eron finally said dryly.

Jovark stopped. After a moment's pause, he approached where she lay, reaching into a drawer on the underside of the bed. "I do not," he said, and produced a shackle that he secured around her right ankle. The metal was thin and light, but strong she could easily tell. Eron sighed dramatically at this stage, but waited as patiently as she could while the captain removed a thin length of silvery chain from the same drawer and fastened it to the shackle. She was now effectively chained to the bed, but she could see the chain's length gave her some range around the room.

Indicating a small room within his quarters he said, "There's a chamber pot behind that little door right there. I realize it may not be the extravagant plumbing your type are used to, but it will serve."

"Indeed," she replied, flexing each hand as he untied the ropes around her wrists. "And am I to remain here for the entirety of the voyage that is to deliver me to slavery?"

"Aye," Jovark said easily.

"Nude?"

"*Aye.*" He smiled, running his hand along the bed's comforter. "It pleases me to find you waiting for me, chained in this fashion to the instrument that bends you to my desires."

Eron shook her head. "I demand clothing."

"I expected as much. You'll not get it." Jovark paused for dramatic effect. "Not unless you're good."

Eron shot him a look, trying a new tack. "And what makes you think I enjoy being good?" she asked with just a hint of husky intent in her voice.

The pirate raised an eyebrow at that, stopped by the promise of her notion. Then he shook his head at her. "I should expect that from a bitch of Capriana."

"I am Eronica, Lady of Tibeth," she told him proudly. "I won't be called a 'bitch' undeservingly."

"Immaterial, *slave*, as all 'Ladies' of Capriana are untrustworthy." His voice was as hard as his voice, and his knuckles whitened on his sword hilt.

"And just what is it you hold against my homeland so harshly, captain?"

Jovark's mood became even cloudier. "The strongest nation in the world? Nothing. I am particularly impressed by the governing Kingdom's ability to defend the people of the lesser kingdoms and isles by simply leaving them to the mercies of Shebwai."

Calmly Eron sat up, trying to straighten her appearance. "That is an interesting notion, coming from a pirate," she said, running her fingers through her tangled hair.

"As I indicated, I do not expect you to understand." His hand went for the door handle as he made to leave the room.

"Where is Corine?" Eron demanded, stopping her captor.

"Your serving girl?" he said wistfully. "Serving my crew, I should expect." Eron could only guess at his meaning, though she hoped it was more in an official capacity than sexually.

"You will see that she is fed and properly cared for, captain."

"Will I?" he asked sardonically. "Lucky for you both that is the case, as I expect to get quite a lot of money for you on the block." His hand turned the cabin door's handle.

"What is your name?" she asked as sweetly as she could manage, attempting to gauge his facets with the change in her own demeanor. "Your full name?"

He turned and gave her a full bow, sweeping his arms in front of his chest. "I am captain James Basil Jovark, My Lady—at your service." Then he gave her that callous grin once more, reminding her of his outward nature's dominance. "Which is a fallacy, as you are now at mine." With that, he left the room at last.

Good morning, captain," came the mumbled greetings from several members of the crew. The command deck afforded them a view of an unblemished blue expanse in all directions.

"Boys," James replied. "Mr. Bevisc,"

"J.J.," Telorn nodded, informally greeting under his breath. "Calm morning. No ships in site, and we're on course for the port at Shebwai."

"How're the men's heads?" James asked with a shake of his own.

"They'll live," the first mate said, rubbing his scalp.

"And the girl?"

Telorn laughed a little. "Agreeable," he chuckled. "By the time most of the men remembered she was there, they were too drunk to do anything about it. A couple stumbled to the hold and managed to undo some of the ropes."

"Mean Ben among them?" James inquired subtly.

"No, cap'n. I had the boys challenge him at cards. It kept him busy till the wine kicked in." For a moment Telorn seemed distracted. "She, uh, definitely seems to have enjoyed her training at whatever Chateau she named as her training ground."

James snorted. "I'm glad to hear it. Well, at least you were keeping an eye on her, as you said."

"Aye, cap'n." Telorn smiled ruefully. "And her mistress?"

James caught himself before he could physically glance back at the doors leading to his cabin.

Eronica—A promising name that only confused the sailing captain further. Certainly the woman's looks had been just as gratifying as he had wished when he had first spied upon her. Moments before, when she had sat up on the bed of his quarters, James had to stop himself from gasping at her beauty. Even after a night's use and then left lying naked in their own sins she could still rise like a vision. Her large, full breasts—flawless in their form and weight—had been openly displayed in their perfection. Her hair had been highlighted in the streaming daylight, the sun's rays playing too off of her ivory skin. Round shoulders supported slim arms and ribs devoid of any ounce of fat. As she had lain beneath him, James had been instantly captivated by the precise curves of her calves, thighs and the roundness of her hips. Her stocking-clad toes had stayed pointed and arched, even as she struggled against the ropes that bound her to his bed and finally his touch. Her breasts had swayed with each thrust into her body, and her face—often as hard as it could be unreadable—eventually melted into a visage of delight. She became a goddess upon an alter of sex, mouthing breathless moans that seemed to say '*Take me*,' despite the means in which he was having her. Truly Eronica was more than he had bargained for.

Attempting to push aside such dangerous thoughts and their eventual conclusions, James reminded himself that she was a cargo, and from Capriana at that. The safety of his men, as always, came first. "*But*," he promised himself, "*I shall have my fun while I can afford it.*"

"Most agreeable," he finally said in answer. "A rare specimen that I think I will savor again."

Telorn grunted approval. "It *is* some time before we reach Shebwai."

"Understood," Jovark said, risking a glance back at his quarters. He turned his thoughts to the ship's responsibilities. "Well, it's time to inspect the rest of the booty. I assume it is down in the hold?"

"Aye," Telorn nodded, "with the serving girl."

She sat alone, attached to the chain that kept her restricted to the hold among the chests, tarps, and single chamber pot that inhabited the room. "You are Corine?" James asked of her as he descended the wooden steps leading to where she knelt.

"Yes," she answered with subdued fear. "Where is my mistress? Is she harmed?"

"No more than yourself," the captain said, regarding her disheveled and somewhat torn garments. The gown she had been brought aboard in had been removed at some point, leaving her in a girdle and shift that hung limp from one shoulder. She knelt in the customary position of supplication, and James knew that the redheaded beauty had indeed been trained at the Chateaus of Capriana. She would bring a handsome price on the Shebwai auction, and might just as easily survive whatever ordeal befell her after that. Slaves were prized high in the dusty, gods-forsaken land that they were bound for. Corine's hair was not as full as Eronica's, nor were her pert breasts of equal size; that much he could tell through the thin shift even in this dim light. But her face was pretty and her body thin and fit, and she bowed her head even when he stepped up to where her knees rested on the wooden floor.

"Are you here to have your way with me as well, sir?" She almost sounded hopeful at the prospect. He doubted that she'd needed much coaxing at the hands of Telorn and the men.

"Tell me of your mistress," James commanded once he was sure that no one was at the top of the stairs listening. When the girl looked up questioningly, he added, "I fear for her prospects in Shebwai, given the willful demeanor she seems determined to show. You seem... better trained."

"Perhaps you simply bring out the best in my mistress." The words had been spoken demurely enough, but they were defiant nonetheless.

"*There* it is," James replied, wagging a finger coupled with a mocking smile at her. "There's that Capriana smugness. It will only cost the pair of you, you know." He turned, pacing the room between the looted crates and chests housed from one wall to the other. "I've no respect for your kind, so you can stop trying to be my equal. Servants both, you and I are, but in very different capacities. You are NOT my equal, of that be certain."

"My Lady is no servant, sir. But if you worry for her safety, you could simply try talking to her."

James cocked an eyebrow at her. "Indeed? And what of you? How will you fare in Shebwai?"

"Sir?"

He leaned in, taunting her with his words. "'Tis a land where women like you are the spoils of war, Corine. Where you are to be taken, beaten when you fail or when your masters simply desire it. A land where you are slave, and not simply servant. If your master is three hundred pounds and never bathes and smells of the desert heat, he will have you anyway, and you must not protest his bulk nor his lack of preening. Do you think a mere waif of Capriana can handle such notions?"

The girl may have been trained, but she still had her naivety. Corine's breathing became labored and her eyes widened, scared by the captain's words. "I won't be sold with the mistress?" she asked, betraying her truest fears.

"Few are so lucky." James angrily waved away the reasons he had come to his ship's hold. These were just foolish girls of the First Kingdom. Why should he care what happened to them? Once more, thoughts of revenge on Capriana's betrayal fueled James's words. "Don't worry, little one; we'll make sure you're properly prepared for what awaits you in the Sultan's land." He strode purposefully up the steps and left Corine below, alone with her thoughts.

Eronica lay sprawled across the bed, cradling her head in the crook of one arm as she cocked one leg to the side. She'd managed to remove the stockings despite the insulting manacle on her ankle, and now she waited on her naked belly for her captor's return.

Eron had almost full range of the room and had used her time to explore the space, checking the drawers for weapons and other items of use. Finding neither blades nor pistols, she could only assume that the captain kept them elsewhere, possibly in the one set of drawers she could not reach while chained or some other locked crevice. Instead she had found expensive baubles and well-designed furniture. She wondered how many of the objects had been loot, and how he'd even acquired such a beautiful vessel in the first place. Fingering each candlestick and inspecting every polished surface, she questioned the fastidiousness of this man. Dirty of the sea, a captain, pirate, and killer, he surrounded himself with beautiful things and left his room tidy. She had shrugged, returning to her search of the quarters.

Only briefly had Eron contemplated the idea of pulling out one of James's coats to cover herself with, but in the end it seemed like such a pointless venture. There was nothing he had not already seen and nothing he would not do to her anyway. She would rather bend him until he gave her back women's clothes, or at the very least she'd give the scheme a try. The coat would have been too hot in the stuffy room anyways.

Eron turned to the largest set of windows and decided to chance working the latch. She had no idea what he might do to her if she broke any part of the expensive stained glass portal, but she wanted to see the outdoors, and let the room air somewhat. She found the mechanism easy and well made, not brittle, so Eron unlatched the windows and pushed them open like a set of miniature stable doors, exposing the churning ocean that extended to the unseen horizon. She stared over the rear of the galleon for what seemed like hours, wondering where, back among the clouds that dimmed so far away, her beloved homeland might be.

Above her position Eron could hear voices of the crew, closer than she would have liked. The prospect of some sailor being able to somehow peer in, or even enter the cabin through that aperture while she was chained in the nude was one she didn't enjoy entertaining. Changing her mind regarding clothes, Eron went back to one of the drawers and took out a simple white poet shirt made of thin linen. Putting the garment on, she found that its hem barely covered the tops of her thighs, but it was better than nothing. Eron rolled up the puffy sleeves and laced the neckline a little to cover her cleavage. The motion was ultimately ludicrous, as her long legs were actually accentuated by the shirt's shortness. She giggled slightly, absently fingering the collar. The initials '*J.J.*' were sown along one hem there.

Captain James Jovark. She laughed at the haughty name, but stopped when the image of his searing eyes burned their way back into her mind. His flesh had been like fire burning against hers, his kiss a conquering sword she had not realized her desire for. But he was still just a rung in the ladder to her goal, and one she must step beyond. Eron knew his touch, though pleasurable, was marred in blood. She decided hating him quietly was an easier course than entertaining more damning ideas. It would be easier to live with later.

Leaning over the side of the bed, Eron ran her fingers along the fine wood. She stopped, her sensitive fingertips finding a slight crease that she had not noticed between the drawers before. When she pressed, a hidden door fell open. Eron smiled at the small victory, and slid off of the covers to kneel beside the tall bed. She reached a slim hand inside the secret hole and pulled out a piece of parchment. The seal had been broken, the document re-folded so perfectly that the wax had nearly melted back to the surface.

Eron opened it carefully, finding an official declaration. Dated five years hence and signed by the King of the Fourth Kingdom himself, it proclaimed *Captain James Basil Jovark as a Privateer in the employ of the Grey Isles*. That the *Angry Goddess* was *a gift, henceforth to be used in ventures that benefited the Grey Isles' interests*.

Well, Eron thought; that explained where he got the ship. It also helped clear up the captain's linguistic skills and apparent tutelage, at least to some degree. The man would have to have been a gentleman of some level—at least at some point in his life—to have been granted audience with the King. With such a strong allegiance to his homeland of the Isles, the document certainly lent some credence to his vehemence towards Capriana, which had been powerless at the time to stop the annexation of the Fourth Kingdome by Shebwai. Still, this was only one part of the picture.

Eron heard familiar boot-steps heading the way of the cabin. She hastily put the document back and returned to her position on the bed.

Again James stopped in his tracks. His captive was face down on his bed, asleep apparently. She had donned one of his shirts, but in her restless dozing the garment had risen, revealing much. He marveled briefly at her form: The supple lines converging at the dip in Eronica's back became the luscious, rounded globes of her ass. Her perfect backside led to those long, coltish legs, slightly askew on his bedspread. The thought of her quim resting against the covers of his bed sent blood rushing to his cock, and he wanted her, then and there.

Waking, Eron simply looked up at him from under dark lashes and cascades of brown hair. Her breasts, barely visible through the linen, rested like billowing clouds upon the horizon of the comforter.

James looked around the room, finding it relatively in order, though the girl had opened the windows. Throwing his coat upon the closest chair, he decided that cooling down was perhaps not a bad idea.

"You wish to have me again?" she inquired when James began to remove his shirt.

"I do," he told her simply. He slipped out of his shirt, trying to appeal to her sexual instincts with a sly look and the slow reveal of some skin. If nothing else, his intentions were being conveyed simply enough.

"And if I refuse to comply?"

Laughing a little, James thought about that with a moment's regard of her figure, then stooped to remove each of his boots. "You have little true say in the matter, though I do not prefer for you t'think of it as another 'rape'."

Regarding the sword, whip, and other weapons that he was laying aside, Eron's mood turned unreadable. Her body's posture was sexually provocative but her facial expression was insolent and stern. "You think you can tame me?" she asked, though the question was not an invitation.

James sighed, sitting in a chair across from the bed. "I think I have a very short time with you, and that we should both enjoy my lenient offers while we can."

"Lenient!" she exclaimed.

"Aye, lenient. How do you think you will be treated in Shebwai, especially in a harem? Furthermore," James continued, stripping off his breeches, "I can make you comply, though I'd rather you simply gave in. I am going to have you, one way or another, so you might as well take pleasure in it."

There was a slight shake of Eron's head. She seemed disappointed by this argument of wills. "You would beat me?"

"I could," James admitted, glancing at the whip he had discarded. "You might as well learn submission now as that is the way in Shebwai. And while my crew has fallen in line with some of their," he paused, mulling the next word over, then spitting it out disapprovingly, "*ways*, I would rather not resort to such actions here, unless needed."

"You don't like them, do you?" Eron observed.

"My crew?"

"No," she replied flatly. "The Sultan's men—nor his ways." When James didn't answer her, she pushed a little more. "Why do you privateer for him, then?"

"I like to be on the winning side."

Studying him a moment, the girl cocked her head to one side and declared, "Bullshit."

She read him better than he would like to have cared, that much was certain. "Alright," he admitted, "I made a deal with him when we were caught by the Shebwai navy." But that was all James was going to admit to her. "My men and I get to keep our lives," he told her, adding, "at sea. In return we prey upon the Sultan's enemies and bring the spoils to him. Given the fact that lands such as Capriana let the Grey Isles fall to Shebwai's might without so much as batting a painted eyelash, I am only so happy to oblige the man."

"You hate him," she seemed to realize, "yet you aid his conquest." Again, James's answer was silence. "You won't admit it to me; fine. Just as you won't admit that you like me and would rather I reciprocated your advances." She raised an eyebrow at him. "Taken with me, are you?"

James's mood darkened, and he stood, exposing his nudity to her as he approached. "You say these things like they matter. I have to sell you once we reach Shebwai—it is as simple as that." He grabbed her chin in his hand, forcing her to look up past his hardening cock into his searing eyes. "All that matters is the fleeting moments of pleasure we're afforded between the daily tortures of this life."

She merely looked up at him from the palm of his rough hand.

"Now, will you submit?"

Eron shook her head at him. "You will not tame me."

"I do not have to tame you." He turned back to his discarded clothes, picking up one of his long belts. James wrapped it around Eron's neck, effectively collaring her. He never released his makeshift leash, but he did produce a key that undid the chain at her ankle. Giving the leash a quick tug, he commanded her to stand. "Come with me."

Eron glared back only a second before rising for her captor. Gripping her slender shoulders, James tore open the shirt she had put on, but it did not even elicit a gasp from her. "I hope you don't expect me to mend that for you," she remarked, indicating the buttons that had ripped free.

"Maybe I do." James turned her around long enough to use a bit of rope to bind her hands behind her back.

"Do you fear I might be able to fight back?"

"I fear nothing," he told her, securing the bindings. "Except my cargo doing something that might damage its worth."

Eron visibly blanched at that. "Where are you taking me?"

"To my ready-room," James said. "It overlooks the deck of the ship."

"And what, pray tell," the girl asked, still sounding unimpressed, "is on the deck of your terrible ship?"

James smiled. "By now—Corine." A look of shock finally passed behind those beautiful green eyes of hers, and he sensed before he felt her tremble slightly. Marching her nude in front of him, James opened the door from his quarters and led Eron down the narrow hall to the door on the left. The naked pair of captor and captive stepped inside the dark room. The taller James could feel his hardened cock graze her hands and backside, even as her fragrant hair brushed his chest. He wanted her and would have her, as he had told her.

"We shall watch my men beat *her* until you comply with my wishes."

Chapter 5

Eron gasped at his words, but he tugged at her makeshift collar again, silencing whatever protest she was about to let slip through. "I told you, Eronica, Lady of Tibeth, you are mine until we reach Shebwai. Capriana has abandoned you. Accept it."

"No," she groaned defiantly.

Wedging his erect manhood in the hollow of her ass, James leaned against her, whispering hotly against the back of her ear. He had pushed her against a low filing credenza along the farthest wall. One long lick between her shoulder blades was enough to make her body shy, bending her forward over the tabletop and pushing her backside harder against his thighs. His hands slid slowly from her writhing shoulders to the large swells of her hanging breasts, though his right never released the belt around her throat. "Get used to submission."

"Not to you."

"Give in," James hissed.

"No."

"Very well," he shrugged, and just before his hands could finally cup her bosom, he used them to push open the shutters of the window over the cabinet. Light flooded the room and Eron, who had been nearly nosed against the shudders found herself suddenly looking out over the deck of the *Goddess*. James smiled and looked over her head at the sight of his crew gathered below them. A holler arose from the crowd when they saw their captain bending the beautiful woman over the view.

At the center of the group below was the mainmast of the ship, and tied to it, with her hands roped above her head and her hair disheveled around the shoulders of her gown, was Corine. The girl was gagged and frightened, but otherwise unharmed—thus far. "Then watch as my crew has its fun."

"You wouldn't," Eron gasped, looking back at him.

Pulling on the leash, James forced her to look down at the scene being played out beneath them. "I wouldn't. But they will."

"Stop this," she choked.

"Give in to me."

Eron paused at last, and James watched her study the horrific tableau of her friend surrounded by the slavering crew.

Ropes encircled the serving girl beneath her breasts and around her thighs. Corine's ankles were spread somewhat, tied at nearly opposing sides of the base of the thick mast, leaving her to some extent off-balance. She struggled against the bonds and looked up at her mistress being nakedly manhandled in the window above.

Mean Ben stood to one side, waiting for the signal to begin beating her with the leather flogger. James's heart almost went out to clueless Capriana girl at the sight of tears falling down her cheeks, but he knew she had been trained for such acts of sexual use. He focused on the feeling of power that he got by bending the most beautiful woman he had ever had over his furniture, anticipating the moment when he could finally plunge his engorged rod into her once more.

"You can't damage your tribute to the Sultan," Eron responded in desperation. Trying to sound angry, she shoved back, eliciting an involuntary groan from James as their skin rubbed further. "You can't devalue your stock!"

"True," he conceded, "but I've entertained the idea of keeping her, secretly. In which case she's mine." James shrugged, sounding as nonchalant about the whole ordeal as possible. The end was a foregone conclusion; it was simply a case of how the events would now play out. "If she's mine, I think I can beat her or give her to my crew. Besides, you know as well as I that the flogger is a light instrument, and that a woman trained at a Kingdom *Chateau* could handle that, as well as the entire crew. But I can always have Mean Ben trade up and use his bullwhip first."

"The Sultan would kill you," Eron tried desperately.

"And as you surmised, I'd just as soon run the Sultan through with a Grahrk harpoon and keelhaul him if I had half the chance. We are desperate men, My Lady. Sometimes we resort to desperate measures."

The woman tried to look back, to look him in the eye, but he tugged the belt around her neck and gripped her bound wrists. "I still don't think you would damage her." Strength had returned to her voice, and the battle of wills was rejoined. "Coward."

Leaning against her to drive home his final point, he brought his voice to a whisper. "You're right; I want my men to survive, so I would not defy the Sultan. But that does not mean I deny them a little fun. Now we can watch them whip your friend and then have their way with her," he said, looking down at the waiting, catcalling crew, "Or you can give yourself to me, now and for the rest of the voyage."

Eron waited a beat before tensely shaking her head. The gesture made her long brown curls bob about her fatally bowed head.

James smiled. "Commence!" he called, and a cheer went up from the crew. Two men rushed at Corine and with their bare hands they tore her gown free of first her body, then from under the ropes that held her to the mainmast. The girl couldn't suppress a scream at the violent gesture, but the gag kept it in check. She was left in a torn and sweaty white shift that hung stretched from her neck, revealing an ample portion of her chest. "Ben!"

"Aye, Cap'n?"

"You may use the bullwhip."

The scarred and ragged-looking crewmember, with his twisted features and hollow eyes smiled. "*Aye*, Cap'n! Ben happily dropped the cat-o-nine-tails flogger and removed his whip from his belt.

Before he could set to, James called, "Start with the shift."

"Aye." The whip lashed out, biting into the white cotton and splitting it along one side. The crew gave a cheer as the torn garment fell open and revealed her perky young breasts. The whip sailed out again, and the experienced marksman again sliced her clothes without yet marring the skin. The tops of Corine's white thighs were now on display, the length of her shift blowing in the sea breeze. Jovark knew that if he let Mean Ben get out of control, that he would happily beat the girl into a bloody mess, but he also knew that Eron would give in before it came to that.

The whip snapped again, tearing away the opposite side of the first strike, then cracked at her hips. The shredded shift fluttered from the ropes that held the now naked and shivering girl. The crew couldn't see enough; they closed in on the spectacle, careful not to get in the way of Ben's whirling weapon. One last blow cut the shreds free of the ropes, and the garment sailed on the wind over the side of the ship.

"Stop him, you bastard!" Eron had said it low enough that only James could hear. He would let her retain that pride.

Before the first strike that would bite into Corine's flesh could be wrought, the captain called out, "Hold!" The crew voiced their disappointment, but it was Ben that had to physically stop himself from continuing when James called the order again. The mean sailor glared up at the pair in the window. "What's it going to be, Eronica?"

The Capriana woman sighed in defeat. Giving him a slight nod, she bowed to his wishes at last. Even the crew, though, saw that slight motion and they cheered at their captain's victory.

"Spare her the whip and close the shutters," Eron whispered to James, and to demonstrate her intentions she actually rested her straining hips against the credenza and spread her feet further apart on the wooden floor. As she rested her face on the candle-stained tabletop, James could only marvel at her with an expression of open surprise and awe.

"You think Shebwai men will forget such disobedience?" Mixed emotions flooded James from unknown sources. He was turned on by the power he wielded over Eron, and wanted her all the more for giving in to him, but he felt pity and caring for her own needs once more. If he had to leave her at the mercy of whoever bought her on the Shebwai block, he wanted her to survive the ordeal, and that required hard lessons. "I'll not close the shutters," he told her, pulling back on the leash. Then, loud enough for the crew to hear, he said "And you will watch as she is flogged after all!"

For the briefest moment Eron flailed in his grip, but he held her fast and forced her head forward, making certain that she witnessed Mean Ben pick the cat back off of the deck and move close enough to Corine to begin lashing her. The first strike whipped across the serving girl's breasts, and she grunted through the gag. The crew marveled at the way each successive blow made her reddening breasts bounce and her nipples harden. Eron froze, somehow captive to the spectacle.

Ben began to use the flogger to attack Corine's thighs, belly, and undefended quim. Meanwhile, James lit a candle above him and closed the shutters enough that his captive could see out, but that the crew could not see in.

His hands began to roam once more, trailing down Eron's back and over the soft globes of her ass. He slipped his fingers between them, finding her pussy moist and hot, despite her sighed protests. Gripping his painfully hard cock, he guided it down against her opening, sliding it along the wet, waiting lips without entering her. "What part of this turns you on, Eronica? Watching your friend get whipped by hungry crewmen, or knowing that I am about to take you?"

"You're a bastard," she whispered.

Using the belt around her neck to choke her slightly as he pulled back, James held the leather length against her clenching hands and agreed. "True. But I am also going to have you." His voice became hard. "Tell me you want it."

Eron could only whimper and shake her head at him, arching as he pulled her leash back while using his feet to spread hers further.

"Say it," he commanded again, rubbing his thick cock against her channel. Out on the deck, another resounding cheer went up from the crowd as Ben whirled the cat along her inner thighs and pussy, bringing the vocal serving girl to her first gagged orgasm. "Say it." James danced his prick between her thighs, just pushing it between the lips of her quivering mound.

Eron moaned. "I—I want it."

"What?" James insisted, barely spreading and entering her with less than an inch of his substantial length.

"I want it," she repeated.

"What do you want?" He held himself there, at the very edge of plunging into her. Ben Began beating Corine's breasts again, so James reached around to pinch Eronica's left nipple. "Say it."

"Fuck me," she whispered in release. "I want you to fuck me."

James slid into her at last and began pumping away. "Say it."

Eron moaned as he slid into her to the hilt. "Fuck me," she cried as James hammered away. "Oh, fuck me!"

Complying happily, James reveled in finally having what he wanted all along. He pulled on the belt like reins, grabbing at her hair and licking her shoulders while he slapped her ass, all while pumping her mercilessly. When he pulled at her nipples again, Eron groaned and twisted, whipping her sweaty hair about her face and leaning back into his embrace to impale herself on him further. She had found that she liked the ways he could command her body to respond, though Eron would never give James the satisfaction of telling him.

Outside on the deck, Ben had found he could contain himself no longer and had dropped his trousers. He slapped the bound Corine with the flogger, apparently knowing his captain would do worse to him if he got any further out of hand. He positioned himself between her bound-apart thighs and stabbed upwards with his discolored cock, humping the serving girl hard and fast. He got in only one or two more flogs across her chest before pulling free of her and coming on her belly. The grunting, glaring crewman clearly enjoyed the site of his seed dripping down her hips. He moved away dumbly, allowing the next crewman access to their new toy.

The scene only seemed to spur Eron on. She became a wild woman in James's grip, wriggling and grunting, driving her hips back into him as he fucked her. She gasped as she choked under his belt and pulled away from him. Then she lifted her backside to him once more, never taking her eyes off of Corine's fate. "Fuck me," she begged again. "Fuck me, my captain!" She commanded and begged all at once.

James pulled free and sent jets of his hot, sticky load flying over Eron's unblemished backside. He panted while he finished, but Eron only writhed and whimpered, seemingly wanting more. "Corine," he thought he heard her breathe, even as the fourth crewman began to have his way with the girl.

Not wanting to disappoint, James grabbed his prize and turned her around, laying her back on the credenza. Her hands still bound behind her back, Eron could only gaze wantonly down her body at him and arch as her legs were left dangling off the edge of the tabletop. Her large breasts fell aside and she closed her eyes, laying back as though to offer her collared throat to his bite. James entered her quickly, pumping away once more.

He grasped the candle he'd lit above them in one hand. James genuinely surprised Eron by tipping it over her and letting the white, hot wax splash onto her skin. Eron screamed, though it was a sound of pleasure as much as pain. As more drops began to encase her swollen nipples in sticky, hardening wax, she groaned louder. James's thumb worked his captive's clit while his strokes became harder.

The captain glanced out the shutters and saw Telorn loosen the ropes holding Corine enough to force the girl to her knees. The used and sticky serving girl, looking tired and beaten, actually smiled as she complied with the mate's unspoken command. She greedily took Telorn's cock into her mouth and began to suck hungrily. Even with her arms still bound above her she leaned her slim buttocks against the mast for leverage. Telorn smiled and pulled his manhood out of her red lips in time to shoot his load across her tongue, cheeks, and breasts. He then tousled her hair and moved aside, letting the next crewmember try the same act.

James watched the wax drip from Eron's flesh and solidify, so he dripped more down her belly and thighs. Soon she was covered in the stuff, and her torso looked as used as the cum-covered serving girl still being fucked on the deck below.

"Oh, gods!" Eron's breathing became harder, and she started to cry out. He dripped fresh wax onto her chest and then onto the nest of hair above her quim. Increasing the speed and intensity of his thrusts, James helped his captive reach her orgasm. The woman screamed, letting fresh tears stain her hot cheeks. Throwing aside the candle and leash, he gripped Eron's ankles and spread her legs, driving his own final thrusts home. James could feel her womanhood's walls close on him, and he pulled out as he groaned hoarsely, gripping his shaft and aiming his second mass of seed onto her soaked belly.

"Yes!" he told her triumphantly.

James stumbled aside, sitting down across from her ravished body. They both sat there, trying to catch their breath. The noise of the crew's party outside had subsided as well.

Standing, he walked over to where Eron still lay sprawled across the tabletop. "Are you alright?" he heard himself ask her.

She nodded, seeming unsure as to whether she wished to meet his gaze. "Corine?" she finally managed.

A quick look out the shuddered window confirmed that the serving girl was still tired and bound, but all right. "She is unharmed. My crew would not have hurt her."

"I wasn't so sure of that," she chuckled.

"Well, Ben's one to fear, but he's still my dog. I make sure of that." Sitting next to her atop the credenza, he reached for a jug. "A drink?" he offered after taking a swig.

Eron tried to roll off of her bound wrists, but couldn't manage the feat. "I would like my hands untied, please."

"I'll think about it," he teased. He helped her down off the table onto her knees, but left her wrists bound behind her back. Tipping the jug to her lips, he helped her drink.

"Help me stand," she told him.

Gripping the belt, he tugged, motioning her to rise. "You can manage," James told her.

Eron leaned away, giving him a look. "I'm not *your* slave, captain. You did not pay for me, and I've had enough lessons in Shebwai's customs for one day, thank you."

Removing the belt from around her neck, James gripped Eron's elbow and helped her stand. "Indeed? Well in that case, the bonds stay until you can completely admit to your fate."

Eron was quiet a moment, studying him with those dark green eyes. She looked like a goddess despite the sweat, wax, and ropes around her wrists. "More," she said, motioning to the jug held limply at James's side. "Please," she added when no action was forthcoming.

James shook his head, lust blurring his vision once more. "Back on your knees."

"I've already told you, no more lessons."

"And I told you," he retorted calmly, "kneel."

She sighed aloud and acquiesced, getting down onto her knees once more. "If it will parch this thirst."

James walked forward with the jug still at his side, but it was his hips he kept in front of her face. His cock was expanding again at the thought of Eron's lips wrapped around it. She looked up at him, waiting for her drink, but he only raised his dark eyebrows at her.

"I meant the bottle," she said sardonically.

"I will slake your thirst," he agreed, "after."

Silently Eron turned her face away from his desire.

"You just don't get it, woman." But the moment was already ruined. Disappointed, his manhood went flaccid once more.

"Take me back to your quarters," she said coldly. "I need to relieve myself."

Eron found herself alone and chained once again, though her wrists were thankfully free and the bed was softer than the wood floor of the ready-room. She had hated to ruin the moment of their mutual satisfaction, but she could not allow that man to demand just anything of her. She wouldn't have it.

Wondering at Corine's fate, Eron absently wiped the remaining flecks of wax off of her skin. The preceding afternoon had been, though she was loath to admit it, one of the most exciting in Eron's young life. Watching Corine bound, whipped and used had been strangely stimulating, and James's lovemaking had once more been forceful and yet somehow tender and considerate. Unable to equate the contradictions that swam in her mind, Eron rolled over on the bed, regarding James's torn shirt. It would provide her nude form at least a little covering, but it smelled like his skin and only added to her confusion. She hated him for being so hard and thoughtless, but she knew that somehow the captain was a slave like her and under different circumstances he could be a proper lover or even an ally.

A commotion arose from the deck, and Eron heard Corine's scream. Franticly, she rushed towards the door, only to have the chain at her ankle pull her short. "Corine," she cried. "Corine!"

She bent down and tried to get her fingers under the shackle binding her ankle. Briefly studying the lock that kept the chain fastened to her, she wondered if she could somehow jimmy it free. The second scream she heard made Eron decide to chance it. Her training at the *Chateau* had showed her how to pick some simple mechanisms, but she needed to find something to get into the lock. Finding a quill on James's desk she surprisingly made short work of the device. Grabbing the torn shirt off of the bed, Eron opened James's cabin door and ran down the hall to the upper deck of the ship.

The sun was setting on the horizon, lending little light to the scenario, but Eron could make out Corine still tied to the mast. Mean Ben was near her, a bullwhip in his dark hands and a jug of wine near his feet. One of the men was trying to pull him away from the cowering girl, but Ben kept knocking the sailor away. "Tis my right!" Ben cried. "I'll have her proper this time, the slut! Just you watch. See what Mean Ben's whip can do to a woman. I'll have her screaming my name and the devil's own when I'm done!"

"Mister Ben!" James's voice cut the din of gathering sailors and made Mean Ben stop in his tracks, his whip raised midair. Eron watched the captain step up from the hold and pull his sword free of its scabbard, tossing the baldric onto the deck.

Eron clutched the scant shirt to her chest and stepped back into the shadows as the captain challenged his second mate. The coming night's winds made the skimpy garment flutter around Eron's hips, but she ignored her own state, worried more about the fate of Corine. The situation became even graver when she saw Ben grasp the hilt of his own sword and advance purposefully towards the captain. The mate's face was a mask of seething rage; a cornered dog that had finally turned on its master and intended nothing less than tearing out his throat.

Eron found herself frightened for the rakish captain, knowing his life was in peril despite his prowess with the blade. When she remembered the true nature of James's intentions, she markedly attributed her concerns as an extension of being fearful for Corine.

The magician had stepped beside the captain quietly and was removing a vial of potion from his robes. "Captain, I could…"

"Step away, Mr. Kloot," James told him. "This is my job."

"You'll leash me away no longer, cap'n," Mean Ben called out in a voice tainted by pure rage. He waved back to the crew who stood watching the spectacle in open wonder. "Your deal with Shebwai and your damned rules! You'll keep none of us from fate or our spoils, ye bastard," he turned to the crew, waving them on to join in his revolution. None of the others moved to stand by him, opting instead to watch the outcome of this battle, but it did not deter Ben from his intent. "No longer!" he bellowed and he hewed at his captain with a viscous looking cutlass, its edge cut jagged by years of hacking away at steel and bone.

James's rapier blocked the savage chop and then parried the following blows to the side. "You're a fool, Ben. Stand down or die; it's the only time I'll say it."

The marred and stained cutlass slashed an answer at James's chest, but the captain stepped aside of the thrust and used the open opportunity to stab his long blade into the right bicep of his mutinous second mate. Ben screamed, but it was a sound of frustration and anger more than pain. If James had expected the wound to slow Ben's facilities, he was wrong, and it nearly cost him his life right then. Ben's sword answered cut for cut, and took James in the arm. He grunted and backed away, blocking the next swing that had been aimed at his neck.

Eron's hands flew to her face, gasping at the site of the terrific duelist being cut and the severe emotion behind Ben's swing. A slick stain of wetness gathered in the black fabric of James's sleeve, and Eron resisted the urge to run to him and inspect the wound. She could only hope silently that it was not a deep enough gash to impede his skills in his defense of Corine. But she worried terribly nonetheless, seeing the captain set his teeth and stance his footing, preparing to end the fight one way or another.

Pressing his own attack, James's blade moved with unequaled speed and agility, and Ben's life was saved only by his ability to match the captain's strength and back away at the same time.

Suddenly desperate, Ben stabbed, trying to break through the captain's assault and pierce his vitals. James pushed aside each stab, then attacked again. Eron watched his rapier move like liquid lightning; it seemed to spell the names of the gods in the faint sunset light still hanging in the air. Suddenly she realized that he had slashed Ben along the ribs and arms. Ben dropped his cutlass, and a final stab to the thigh felled him to his knees where he waited, panting and groaning in rage.

"Kill me then, ye bastard!"

"I swore an oath," James told him through ground teeth. His blade was drawn back for the killing blow, but his own words stayed his hand. "I'd protect this crew, even at the cost of our own freedom." He lowered his sword, and motioned to the bleeding man. The first mate and another crewmember moved to help the vanquished traitor to his feet. "As that is the only thing I can still take away, that will be your penance. Mr. Bevisc!"

The first mate nodded, holding a cringing Ben aloft by one crimson-soaked arm. "Aye, cap'n?"

"How much time will we lose if we divert to the closest isle?"

Shaking his head, the mate looked dubious. "I'd have to double-check the charts, J.J., but it would be close as hell gettin' back to Shebwai in time. The Sultan will kill us all if we're late."

"And he'll kill Ben for sure if we surrender him to Shebwai." James dropped his bloodied rapier next to where he'd left his baldric on the deck. "I'll kill him myself before I allow that. Rig every yard of cloth and triple-check your charts, Telorn. We exile our traitor within a day or we all hang together, is that understood?" He lowered his voice and looked away. "Take the traitor to the brig and see to his wounds."

Eron had been able to stand it no longer. She took the steps down to the deck two at a time and reached Corine's side, stroking her red hair and asking her if she was all right.

"I'm fine, mistress," Corine answered in a whisper. "He was just... he was going to hurt me. I could see it in his eyes."

Eron freed the girl from the mast, caring little for any reprisal from their captors. She looked up and found James walking intently towards her. Eron quickly stood, trying to look as defiant as possible in her skimpy clothing.

"What are you doing out of the cabin?" the pirate demanded under his breath. He gazed at his crew, but they paid little mind to the captain's women troubles after the duel they had just witnessed.

Relaxing a little, Eron reached instinctively for James's wounds to inspect them. "I heard Corine scream. I'm afraid I could not help myself." She looked him in the eyes for only a moment, seeing little definable message in their dark depths. One thing was for certain; he didn't want to let on to the crew that his charge had somehow escaped her chains. "You're hurt," she heard herself say, trying to change the subject.

"I've had worse."

"Of that, I am certain," Eron agreed, regarding his scars as her fingers pulled aside cleaved cloth and trailed over his muscles. She lingered, unable to tear her eyes or her hands from his warmth. "Calm yourself, captain. If my actions have earned your wrath then subject me to reprisal later. Firstly, you need stitches, and my servant..." She paused, retracting her commanding stance and remembering her current place aboard his ship. "And Corine needs attending."

James had been staring at her the entire time. He fingered his torn shirt when her hands finally left him, looking down to where she had been exploring. "Of course." His demeanor calmed and he seemed to look on her in a new light, taking in her supple form so accentuated in the short, open-front shirt. The wind blew locks of her long brunette curls towards him, and he took a wisp between his thick fingers. "I trust that if I allow you to take the girl to my cabin you will both await there without any fool-hearty actions?" When Eron nodded, James laughed a little as if to say, *what am I to do with the pair of you?* "I'll be up soon. See to the girl's needs, our own surgeon will see to mine."

Eron led Corine away, wrapping a blanket around the shivering girl's naked shoulders. When she looked back to where she had left the captain standing, she found him watching her in turn.

Chapter 6

My Lady?" **Corine** held Eron close and ran her hand gently up and down her back. Eron held back the tears as best she could, but already she was letting her strong-willed resolve slip in favor of mutually needed comfort. Corine held her in her arms and said nothing of the shudder in her mistress's voice. "What is it? Please, tell me."

"I just," Eron bit her lip, holding back the tears again before continuing. "I just wish I could find a different way through this. None of it is how I expected things to be. It is all so much more complicated."

Corine's voice was strong, but she kept almost at a whisper as she cradled the other woman. "What did you expect, mistress? Things are never how we imagine them, especially where danger is involved."

"But I should have realized things would be layered. Instead I let my anger for how Shebwai's armies were changing our home spur us both into danger. I made up my mind long ago that every man we would meet on this quest would be a blighted blaggard. From the Sultan, to the soldiers and slavers,"—she paused, uncertain of what she was admitting to her friend—"right down to the pirates; that they would all be simple, evil men with black hearts. Now my feelings leave me weak and we are both lost if I let that happen."

"The captain," Corine inquired, "what has he done to you?"

Eron waved the inference away. "Oh, nothing I cannot handle. It is just that I know that there is more to this man than a simple privateer in the Sultan's employ. He does things that I cannot condone, and yet I begin to understand his plight and… and I sympathize for him."

"He spared the man that would have beat me," Corine agreed without malice, "while still saving me from true harm. He has honor, caring for his crew despite their actions."

"He has honor simply for his own, yet he was once a kingdom man himself." Eron's voice turned harsher, and she wiped away the tears that had welled in her eyes. "And he hates those of the kingdom for leaving his people behind to become slaves and pirates."

Corine leaned Eron back so that she could look in her eyes again. "He hates my Lady?"

Eron smiled, but there was no humor in it. "He wants to, but like me I think he sees something more than a simple victim. Even when he is rough with me, his touch is like nothing I have known before. He holds back from the harshness he could inflict, as though treating my body like a lover's, not a slave's. His kisses are deep and powerful, and his hands work magic that no spell could truly elicit."

"You are taken with him," Corine said without question.

Shocked, Eron stared openly at the maidservant for a silent moment before sighing and letting her long hair shade her turned-away face. "I am taken with his plight, and the kind of man he could have been, were circumstances different."

Corine rubbed her mistress's shoulders. "The crew used me as a slave girl, but they not did bear me true malice, save for the one called Ben. Some of them were once civilized men, I can see now." She smiled a little, biting her lip. "The mate, the one called Telorn; he is an experienced lover."

Returning the knowing grin, Eron raised an eyebrow. "Oh?"

"He commanded me," she reminisced, "and willed me to pleasure that satisfied us both, and he was never unpleasant." She paused, thinking quietly with a faraway glance that Eron could not read. "They were kingdom men, you said?"

"Of the Grey Isles," Eron nodded. "This ship once sailed in the King's service, but was taken by the Sultan's navy some years hence, as were their homelands." Eron's voice became hard again, and she suppressed the urges that had brought her to her current predicament, swallowing her hatred down to a cold, festering place. "Captain Jovark seems to have made some plea for his crew's life, but it has meant sailing against the ship's of the world, Kingdom or otherwise."

"That does not mean that they could not be convinced to be allies," Corine said with breathy empowerment.

"Perhaps," Eron agreed. But it would be a hard argument to back at this stage, and within a few days I think we'll be in Shebwai. And then our troubles really begin." Desperate fear threatened to again steel away Eron's resolve, and she fought to put such terror aside, hopeful that her last hours aboard the *Angry Goddess* might be pleasurable, at least. She removed her single garment and moved to bring over a water basin. "Come on. Let's get you cleaned up."

James breathed a concealed sigh of satisfaction when he opened his cabin door and found the two women asleep on his bed. They were nude and entwined in each other's limbs, the girl resting her head on Eron's bosom like a child. The torn shirt his captive had been wearing lay in a crumpled, ripped heap at the foot of the bed, having obviously been used to clean the redhead and mop her troubled brow. The captain regarded the redundant chain that lay near the shirt, wondering only briefly as to how his captive had escaped it. It mattered little, he knew, just as he realized it would do little good to affix the chain again unless he was going to bind the woman's hands, and he had no need of that right now. Feeling strangely compassionate after the sentence he'd had to pass on his second mate, he regarded the two sleeping beauties once more before quietly exiting and closing the door behind him, leaving them alone.

The wounds ached, but James could easily move and flex regardless of the mystical stitches Jack Kloot had affixed. Hating pain, the captain sought out Telorn and whatever ale he might have handy.

"A difficult night," Telorn Bevisc said when the captain found him at the bow of the ship. He handed his friend a bottle.

"Aye," was all James could find to say.

"For centuries, sailors have believed a woman aboard ship to be a curse." Telorn shrugged, taking a swig. "We knew things would deteriorate, but even I did not expect things to get bad this fast."

James scowled at his mate's inference. "We've had women aboard before."

"I was not referring only to Ben," the mate retorted with a look.

"The others are angered over today's events?"

Telorn shook his head. "No, J.J. They are loyal. But Ben's fate is hard to take, even knowing his nature as they do. It's the circumstances that have led to this day. How long can we go on like this? I knew Ben would be the first to crack, but…" He trailed off, taking another drink of the rum. "And what about you? Has she gotten too close?"

Shooting his subordinate a stern glance, James quickly relented, realizing Telorn was voicing his fears also as a friend. "I admit, this life is a hard one, and I long perhaps for other things. The woman has… spirit."

"They both do."

It was James's turn to regard his friend with surprise. "Gotten to you, has she? The little one?"

Telorn smiled and shrugged. "I simply miss the company of Kingdom women sometimes, and the serving girl reminded me why."

Exhaling deeply, James's shoulders drooped. He leaned on the rail of the *Goddess* and watched the night sky through the haze of alcohol. "I did not want to admit such things, but you are right. The others can only feel the same. We are not free men, to go where we please or take up our own lives, no matter how we fool ourselves by being out here on the sea."

"The sea is where we belong," Telorn reassured. "You did what you could to keep that in our lives. But no, this is not freedom."

"It'll be worse for them," James remarked, tossing his head back at where his cabin waited.

Telorn nodded once more, tossing his bottle over the side. "And there is nothing we can do."

Land ho!" **Jack** Kloot lowered his magician's spyglass, and called the announcement down from the crow's nest again in confirmation. "Mr. Bevisc was right, captain. 'Tis little more than a sandbar and a ring of trees, but I see some water and fruiting bushes."

"We can reach it within an hour and be back on course," James muttered to Telorn. He looked up at the climbing sun of the morning before regarding his mate's charts. "They're going to be pissed; we *will* be late."

"You'd have it no other way, J.J.," Telorn reminded him firmly. "I'm sure we can find some excuse for being late, despite the fair weather we've had for," he laughed a little, "well, for weeks."

"Indeed." James returned the laugh. "Fuck the Sultan. He can believe my reasons for being a day late, or he can rot."

"You can fuck the Sultan, if it means the rest of us don't get hanged," Telorn said with a sardonic smile. "I'd rather stick to women. Speaking of such carnal desires, where has our best cargo gone?"

"My cabin," was all the captain would admit, still unsure how Eron had escaped the lock on her manacle. "I should check on them before we reach the island."

James opened the door to his quarters, finding the two women apparently in the midst of a game of 'dress-up.' They were each in various states of dress, having found a number of women's gowns in the wardrobe furthest from the bed and dumped several of the dresses onto the floor, mixing and matching portions of each. The paused in mid-laughter, affixing their captor with surprised looks before bursting again into hilarity. For an instant, James felt embarrassed, then angered at himself for allowing the women such a freedom, given that his weapons were stowed behind the other door of the wardrobe, albeit locked. He tossed both emotions aside and simply rolled his eyes at the giggling ladies, moving to help them pick some of the gown bits off of the floor. "I see you are in better spirits, this morning."

"Aye, cap'n," Corine managed before spluttering anew. Eron covered her mouth, trying to suppress her own urge, but soon joined her maidservant in open laughter.

"You can keep the shift," he told her, fingering Corine's 'gown' briefly before motioning to the wardrobe. "But the rest you do not need until tomorrow."

"Oh," Corine pouted, removing her clothing and whining further when the captain turned her back to him and tied her hands.

"Leave us," he told her with a point of his chin towards the deck. "Find the first mate. He'll attend to your *needs*, I'm sure, my Lady."

"Ooh, Aye-aye, cap'n," she responded, eliciting a new, though subdued, round of laughs. She left the cabin and managed to close the door despite her wrists being bound at her back.

James turned on a suddenly quiet Eronica. Trying to keep the mood light, he flashed her a quick smile. "Remove the gown, Eron. I would share some pleasure before this day's work must commence."

She simply stood there, clad in four mismatched colors, looking at him.

James glared, and then he guffawed a great belly laugh, doubling over as he pointed at her.

"What?" Eron asked after enduring the mocking for a few moments, clearly perturbed.

Wiping fresh tears from his eyes, the captain took in her silly costume and shook his head. "You look like a deranged rooster."

Eron's lips became a thin line and she crossed her arms over her proud chest. "Perhaps it is the fashion this year in the Kingdoms."

James laughed. "I doubt it seriously."

"And how would you know?" she challenged. "You could have taken the *Goddess* to safe territories at any time; Morbindar, Valiende, the Fields of Cane. No. Instead you loot the seas for the Sultan's gain."

"Leaving the crew's families in the Grey Isles to be butchered as the price of our freedom, should we have ever decided to run." James's mood had turned instantly, and he fixed her with a commanding glare that he hoped she would back down from before she enraged him any further. The stresses of recent days had been enough to push him without this sort of retaliation, much less his own crew beginning to feel the noose tightening. He averted his eyes for just an instant, trying to calm them both. "Will you remove your clothes or not?"

"I will not be commanded."

"And I will not be challenged by the likes of a spoiled Capriana bitch!" He advanced on her, obviously surprising her with his ferocity when he grasped Eron's shoulders and pulled her to him. He tore her bodice free, the unlaced garment coming away without a fight.

She stood frightened and awed by his anger, defiant in a shift and layered petticoats. "We are all slaves, captain," she managed. "At least I fight for my liberty."

Dropping the pouches and tankard off of one belt loosed from his hips, James used the long leather strap to tightly bind Eron's wrists and tie them above her head to the top of one post of his bed. "You fight me," he pointed out, "here. But should you continue this futility in Shebwai you will have it ten times worse." He pulled at the belt again, raising her strained wrists so that she was forced to her toes, wincing. "The men of Shebwai train their slaves. Beat them if they fail, break them when they succeed," he yanked her petticoats to the floor, "and kill them if they will not break." He tore open the shift's neckline, exposing her raised, heaving breasts. James clenched one in his large hand while seizing her jaw-line with the other. His lips mashed down on hers and he felt her breath explode into his mouth with a slight mew of resistance when his tongue invaded her recesses. He was working himself up to having her, teaching her that she had no hope in Shebwai as a Lady, even if it meant raping her with open contempt.

Her kiss stopped him when, for an instant, they both forgot his intentions and let their tongues intermingle. She gave a breathy moan into his mouth, then turned her head away when he stopped. James pulled back, disgusted with the whole scenario. He wanted to tell her that she'd never learn, and would die at some desert rat's hands for it. He wanted to tell her she deserved better, or that she should never have come out from under the protective blanket of a blissfully ignorant Capriana. Instead he just grunted and turned his back on her in frustration, leaving her tied to his bed's post, her chest heaving and her face a mixture of want and contempt.

James stormed onto the deck in time to see the beach rolling into view. "Where's that damned traitor bastard?" He demanded aloud to anyone who would hear. "Have him brought forth!"

Two crewmen dragged a bandaged and bound Ben out for their captain, forcing him to kneel. Others were lowering a boat to the waterline, ready to take their former second mate to his exile.

"Mean Ben," James invoked. "You are sentenced to exile for crimes against the captain of the *Angry Goddess* and her crew. All here should be reminded by this event that no man's needs here are above or below his fellow's own. Equals we have been in our curse since becoming bound to Shebwai, but equal to us you are no more. You'll be left to the elements of that nameless isle, Ben, with naught but a blade and the clothes on your back for your crimes. Your offense will be hidden from Shebwai in hopes that your loved ones will not pay any further price for your failures as a man." Sternly, the captain pointed one finger at the island and looked down at Ben for the last time. "Take him away!"

The men grabbed up the beaten sailor. "I'll kill you for this, ye bastards," Ben cursed as he was dragged to the boat.

"Wait," James commanded. He reached for the coiled length of Ben's bullwhip, left sitting next to the mainmast. Handing it to one of the crewmen taking Ben ashore, he leaned in so that only the condemned might hear. "For your troubles. If it becomes too unbearable, it would make a good noose."

As the dingy was rowed to the island Ben's voice became a harsh, far off roar until finally he was pulled forcibly onto its beaches. One man pointed a pistol at the exile's head while another cut his bonds, then both abandoned him there to his own devices as they got back into the boat and rowed away.

By the time the dingy returned, the *Goddess* was already turned for the open sea again, and Ben was a pathetic black dot lost on a field of white sand.

"Make for Shebwai, with all speed," the captain told the helmsmen, though the anger had at last fled from his voice. The emotion had been replaced by another James had long thought he'd abandoned; remorse.

Three silent hours of travel had passed since leaving Ben behind, but James stood rooted still beside the ship's wheel, watching the open sea ahead.

"Change of watch," he called out suddenly, and the equally quiet crew changed posts and replaced the hardest-worked with those that had been resting. Jack Kloot came down from the rigging where he'd diligently watched the horizon since before sunup. He paused to say something to his captain, but thought better of it when he saw James's expression. Turning away, he left the post above unmanned, the new man having yet to appear for his posting—a miscalculation James would later attest to his mind being elsewhere.

Five minutes later, Kloot's replacement for the crow's nest was just beginning to climb when the whole ship rocked.

"What the hell?" Startled into action, James held one rail as he looked for the source of the attack. A splash along the port side clued him in to the culprit. His fears were confirmed when the next splash brought the Grahrk's coils high alongside the ship, bumping its hull again.

"Break out the harpoons!" Suddenly the crew was abuzz with need and action, and Telorn was at the captain's side. "Think it followed us?"

James threw his baldric and rapier aside, grasping a cutlass from a sword rack next to the wheel. "It is as if the damn beast knows our best harpoon-man has just been dropped ashore."

The giant, snake-like creature's head reared forth from the churning waves, shaking loose torrents of water. It bellowed a terrible roar as it stared the terrified crew down from eyes like huge, black pools. Some of the men took up the whale spears and readied for a throw, one even taking a shot as he was closest to one portion of the creature's long body. The harpoon bounced harmlessly of off the beast's ringed scales.

"Wait for my command," James ordered. "You're to hit its vitals or you'll do no good!"

The creature took the moment that the crew paused in inaction to reach out with its bearded maw and snatch a sailor off of the foredeck. The man had barely a moment to scream before he was bitten in half. The Grahrk's head reared back, allowing it to swallow what it had taken, then it dipped back beneath the waves.

"It'll come again," Telorn called out. "Aim for its eyes!"

A great crash spilled the crew to a man onto the decks as the ship listed aside and her bow nearly dove beneath an oncoming wave. James looked back to the origin of the collision, finding the creature had retreated back behind the stern and rammed. Splinters of flying wood accompanied the sound of cracking boards as the beast's sheltered head worked whatever damage to the back of the ship it had begun. For a brief moment, James wondered how to even get to the Grahrk much less fight it off.

Then he heard Eronica's scream.

James burst into the halls leading to his cabin, then rushed inside his quarters, a sword in one hand and a harpoon in the other. The scene that met his eyes surprised even the experienced captain.

The rear of his room had been ripped away at one corner, and the snapping jaws of the Grahrk threatened to enter through the breach. The creature's coils had thrown much of the sea into the room, dousing the still-bound Eron's torn shift in water, making it transparent. She struggled against her bonds, staring first at the creature that threatened to eat her, then at her captor, who had left her in her helpless state. She screamed again when the Grahrk's head snaked into the room and made straight for the bed.

Eron pulled at the leather belt above her. She tried to twist her body away from the oncoming sea-creature, but the Grahrk's weight on the rear of the ship was dipping her towards it to the point where she was nearly dangling over its gaping jaws. She screamed again, perhaps happy now that James's binding abilities were up to snuff.

The harpoon James loosed sailed past her and jammed between two of the beast's elongated teeth. It was enough to briefly stop its advance, but as it fell away from its snapping maw, obviously not enough to turn the beast away for good.

James was suddenly there, standing in front of Eron with a saber raised defiantly. She nearly cried in delight at the scene, feeling safe with his body there to defend hers. "C'mon, ye beastie," he challenged aloud. "Tis you and me, now, and you'll not have her. She's mine!"

The creature's head shot out to snatch him up, but James's cutlass caught it in the nostril, the closest open orifice the short blade could reach without its wielder being skewered by the Grahrk's fangs. The serpent reeled back, blood pouring from the fresh wound, but it did not retreat from the cabin. Just before it could attack again, a harpoon sailed past both captive and captor and stuck in the Grahrk's eye. It screamed, slamming its head into the floor and walls of the room as it tried to shake the spear free while backing its body out again. When it finally disappeared from view, Eron chanced a look behind her and found Telorn and some of the crew holding the harpoons that had finally saved her life. When she looked at James she almost laughed aloud at his equally grateful expression.

Soaked to the skin by the creature's attack, Eron writhed against the tightening leather holding her wrists. The movement left little of her scantily clad body to the crewmen's imaginations, and there were a few minutes of staring at her beauty before the sailors finally quit the cabin at Telorn's insistence.

"Cut me down," Eron groaned, the bindings threatening to cut her hands free of her arms. "Please."

James regarded her for a moment, his sword slung over his shoulder as he appreciated her form regardless of his destroyed room. "Are you alright?"

"I will be if you remove this damned wet leather, captain," she pleaded. "*Please.*"

His cutlass made short work of the strap holding her, and Eron fell into his arms. They shared a quiet moment there together as he held her, the only sounds the rolling sea without and their hearts within. Finally he took her chin in his hand and kissed her lips. "Call me James," he told her quietly.

"James?" she smiled.

"Uh huh," the captain nodded. "My friends call me J.J."

Chapter 7

For the briefest moment, Eron actually wondered if she had been dreaming.

She awoke in a dry bed on clean sheets in a quiet room, but the roll of the sea still displaced her balance and she was quite naked, though covered by a soft comforter. When she realized James was standing beside the bed, she reached out and took the plate he had offered.

"A quiet night—now," James commented. "Far cry from earlier."

"Where are we?" Eron wondered aloud. She had apparently passed out in her rescuer's arms and been taken to this place.

"Another cabin," he shrugged. "I figured I'd offer you a dry place to sleep tonight. It's the least I could do." His tone had become quieter—more somber, as though events and emotions of the preceding hours had drained all anger or passion from him.

"Thank you," she agreed, and set to the food with a barely concealed voraciousness. "Aren't you eating?" she asked once she realized she was alone in her consumption.

"I've no appetite, really." He shrugged off her studious look at the admission, busying himself with the lighting of more candles in the room's corners.

Eron decided to press the matter, though she kept her smile sympathetic. "You seem a changed man, captain."

"Nothing that wasn't there before," he defended. "It's all just taken a bit of the wind out of my sails, that's all."

"Complicated, isn't it?"

James came to sit beside her on the bed, taking a strawberry between his fingers and holding it out for her. He teased her lips lightly with its texture before popping it into her mouth. "More complicated than I would like to admit." He averted his gaze, speaking to her with a tone of fact, tainted perhaps by a far-off regret. "The *Angry Goddess* is a ship under rule of the Sultan of Shebwai's navy, Eron," he admitted. "We were captured two years hence, and given the ultimatum to sail as privateers against all enemies of Shebwai, or die. As insurance of our complacency, any families back in the now-occupied kingdom lands we hail from are now under threat. The *Goddess* must return with whatever booty she takes by certain dates, or the families are to be killed and the Shebwai navy will set sail to hunt us down and sink us."

Eron expressed her understanding with a sigh. "Your family?"

"I've had no family except the men I've sailed with since I was a boy," he told her simply. "It's the lads and their lives I think of."

"So tomorrow we reach port in Shebwai, or all is lost." Her hand strayed to his, gently touching his sun-bronzed knuckles. "You could not lead any of us to freedom if you wanted to."

"Tomorrow we put in to Shebwai a day late," James admitted with raised brows. "Thanks to Ben's side-trip to exile. Though we've been late a day or so before. Once we reach port, I'll have to explain our tardiness to the harbormaster as well as whatever search party comes aboard. They'll be making certain we are not hoarding any gold, trinkets or slaves that we may have taken in our travels as 'pirates of the high seas.'" He met her eyes with his own, and though his face was a mask the pain of his responsibilities was evident behind those dark orbs. "I may seem like a free man amongst the wind and waves, but I too am a slave, Eron."

"As must I be after tomorrow," she agreed, "or 'tis death for us both." Longing filled Eron. Equating her emotions for the captain with the simple need to be touched tenderly before her next captivity, she threw caution to the winds of the sea and reached for James. Her hand brushed his cheek as she leaned in to kiss him deeply. "Perhaps things will change soon," she ventured, brushing her lips against his.

If he was surprised by her change in demeanor, he did not show it. "I doubt it," James answered quietly. For a moment Eron wondered if his melancholy might tear him away from her embrace. Instead his grip on her became suddenly firm. "But if I can't have you forever, I'll make certain I brand you this night," he said, punctuating such passionate words with an equally fiery kiss.

Eron wrapped her arms tightly around his neck, diving into his hold with abandon. "I want you, James," she breathed. "Make me yours."

His hands found her hips, nearly tickling the hollow beside the bone with the pressing of his thumbs. They trickled up her naked back, then wove into her hair and pulled her head back from his hungry mouth. He looked at her for an instant, held there by his grip, and then he dove back into her flesh. Running his tongue up the length of her neck, he captured an earlobe in his teeth and breathed against it, making Eron's back arch and a slight squeal of delight escape her throat. James's hands found her breasts and began to knead and squeeze the large globes, making Eron moan aloud at the exquisite sensation.

"Oh, gods, yes," she said hoarsely, her own hands finding the hem of his shirt and pulling it up the length of his toned abs to the hair on his chest. "Ugh, these damned clothes. Why are you still wearing them?"

James laughed and stood, pulling the shirt from his body. Eron sat up and began working at the belts around his narrow hips. She dropped the offending articles to the deck and pulled at the waist of his breaches, lowering them to his thighs much to the captain's obvious delight. His cock sprang forth, already hardening. Eron looked up and returned James's smile before taking the tip of the erect phallus into her mouth. He gave a low groan as she sucked more of him in, then all but gasped as she ran her tongue along the underside as she let him slide back out from between her lips.

Bypassing the length, Eron licked his thigh, the base of his cock, then his swollen balls, letting her tongue's tip reach low behind the warm pair before taking one between her hot lips. She teased and sucked at James before again licking the entire length of his shaft as a prelude to swallowing him whole. As his swelling member filled Eron's mouth and throat, she held him by the base to feel the low rumble of his deep voice as he grunted each new tone of excitement. His hands laced into the tresses of her hair and drew her head back, then pushed it forward again to deeply gobble up his length again. Eron followed his direction, beginning to drag her lips down over him faster, quickening the sweet suckling with each bob of her head.

James hands roamed along her neck and jaw, caressing her hollowed cheeks and smoothing back her hair. He gripped her dark locks again and groaned when her sucking motions became faster and deeper still, and he began thrusting slightly into her mouth. "Yes, Eron. Faster." She did as he asked, letting her teeth rub along the underside of his cock. He gave a slight "Ah," but she knew the pain was light. "Gods," he repeated when she wouldn't let up. "Gods, you know how to thank a man for saving your life."

Eron bobbed her head with increased speed, driving her lips down the length of his cock and working his thighs with her fingertips. "Put your hands behind your back, Eron," he commanded, though it was not as a captor would say it.

She complied, clasping her hands at the small of her arched back as she knelt before him and paid homage to his throbbing phallus. Eron glanced up between licking and sucking him to watch him drink in the sight of her yielding like that, knowing that her hair swayed over the top of her naked ass with each hungry dip of her head.

"Oh, *Gods*."

She could feel him swell in her mouth, readying to cum at last. She worked him all at once with every nuance of her mouth and teeth, driving him deep into her throat while licking and slurping to bring him to climax. He gave way finally, but she did not pull free of him, instead allowing him to spurt his seed deep within. She swallowed each drop greedily, reveling in the hot, salty desire that slid down past her tongue. She let his cock slide free, slowly licking at the remaining drops on the tip playfully.

"That's for saving my life," she conceded sweetly into his ear as he lay beside her.

"Oh?" James rolled over on top of her and took one nipple between his teeth and bit her slightly. "Let me return the favor."

Sliding down to wedge his broad chest between her thighs, James's lips teased the underside of her breasts and the taut lines of her abdomen as she lay beneath him. When he slid further down and enslaved her quivering, wet mound with his mouth, she knew she wouldn't last long. "Yes, James. Yes!"

His tongue parted her moist lips and lapped at her juices, sliding into her womanhood briefly before finding the hardened nub of her clit and tumbling it insatiably. Eron gripped the sheets beneath her as though to hold on for dear life while he made her ride to the next plateau. When he worked his fingers into her and began thrusting, Eron could take it no longer. "Gods!" she screamed as she came, making the already slick pumping of James's fingers even wetter. Not letting up, he lapped the new juices directly from her womanhood, drinking her into a second climax that left her twisting and moaning in his grip.

Still reeling from the effects, Eron could only watch through heavy eyes and panting breath as James positioned himself above her and entered, thrusting his hard rod deep into her soaked flesh. He leaned back, grasping her nipples with his fingers and alternating twists and pinches while he began pumping his cock in and out. Eron went mad with desire, releasing her grip on the bed to toss her wet hair about or grab his muscled shoulders and chest. She gripped his thighs with her calves, but James sat back and spread her ankles wider still. Eron ran with it, wetting her fingers on her hot tongue to rub her own clit and pull at the peak of her right breast.

"Ungh," James groaned louder. He expanded within her, filling her womb, and Eron knew he was ready to cum. She worked her own clit faster, determined to climax with him. She didn't have to labor at it long. Her third pinnacle began to wind within her at the touch of her own hand mixed with the hard, fast thrusts of her lover, spurring him on. James released, groaning aloud as he came within her. He leaned down, taking her free nipple between his teeth. The bite was all it took to send Eron over the edge. She convulsed around him, milking his cock free of every drop of his seed. The captain collapsed atop her, pulling free after a short, warm time of lingering within her. Eron felt the mingling juices slide down between them and smiled at the experience shared.

"Well," she breathed heavily against his long waves of hair, "That was fun."

James laughed a little and began caressing her body to calm them both. After a time, lying there naked and letting the sweat cool their bodies, Eron began to doze. More than she had been with previous lovers, Eron was satisfied, and the thought was almost strange to her. Setting such concerns aside, she decided that she was simply happy to be in the arms of her captain.

Eron found James still beside her when she awoke from a blissful sleep. She did not stir, but opened her eyes to the sight of his calloused index finger delicately winding a lock of her hair into a tight curl. He must have been lying there, watching her sleep as he did this for hours, for when he released the captive lock it stayed in a swirled ringlet.

"Hello," she greeted with a smile. The sun had risen, eclipsing the twin moons and the passion they had wrought. "Enjoying our last moments together?" she asked seriously though quietly.

James ran his thumb along Eron's lips to still her. "Why must you speak of such things?"

"Because the reality of the moment is here," she said. Eron—torn between the feelings she had for him and the mission she was bound by—knew she had to make her point now if she ever hoped to see this man again. "Shebwai calls, and I am to be sold."

"And we are back to being slaves both," James answered, sounding depressed.

"No one need be a slave," Eron told him succinctly.

Narrowing his gaze, James's voice became graver. "That is a strange thing to hear coming from a woman I am about to send to the block."

Eron weighed her words. "What would you do if war came to Shebwai? If the Kingdoms fought back at last and reclaimed the Grey Isles and set your crew's families free?"

"Then I would sail as a free man," he answered with an air of disbelief. "Or I would get drunk, not believing it were true."

"Would you find me?" she asked, cutting off his listless air.

James lost his cynicism completely. "You? You I would search for, Eron. I've never met another woman like you. Smart, beautiful, sexual…" He ran his knuckles softly along her jaw and started playing with her hair again. "If Capriana ever found honor again, then I would find you and return you to her—for a ransom, of course." They both laughed at the light jest.

Eron slid from under the covers at last, exposing her full breasts to his gaze as she sidled against him to nuzzle his unshaven neck. "Do pirates know honor?" she jested.

"I was not always a pirate," James muttered low. "A gentleman with some semblance of pride is given command of a galleon of the Kingdoms. They don't hand out such honors to just any gutter rat."

Eron laughed and held him to acknowledge his words. "Then remember pride and honor, captain. One way or another," she added with meaning, "eventually you are going to have to fight back or die."

Resisting her embrace James grabbed her shoulders to make her look him in the eye. "If you fight your masters in Shebwai, Eron, then you will die," he said, still trying to make her understand.

It broke Eron's heart at that moment not to tell him the mission she was on.

"I won't die, James," she told him, laying her head down in his arms. "I am going to set us free."

He didn't ask her what she meant by that. James could see the feelings in her eyes, so he leaned down to kiss her again. Before the ardor could even begin, there was a knock at the door and the sound of the first mate's voice. "We're coming up on Shebwai harbor, captain," Mr. Bevisc said. "The escorts are nearly on us."

"I should run out the guns," James muttered angrily, though only Erin heard him. "I could sink three of their number easily before they overtook us, by the gods."

"It's nice to hear," Eron whispered, "but not today. Today we would both die. See to your crew, James."

Bolstered by her words, he agreed silently. "Understood," he called to the mate. "Standard approach, Mr. Bevisc. I'll be on deck shortly."

Sighing, he kissed her once more and his lips were strangely soft, his tongue slow and moist within her mouth. It was the kiss of a lover, not a captor. "I don't know what to say," he admitted after a silence. "That's never happened to me before—I always know what to say."

"No words, James. We both need to get ready, before we're boarded." She kissed him again and left his side, looking towards her responsibilities instead of dwelling on the moment any longer. To do so would have brought tears to her eyes at last, and she'd not let him see that. "Let me dress in whatever you need to send me off in," she told him when he didn't rise with her. "But don't let them bind me. Today, only you get to do that."

Nodding once, James got out of bed and found a set of shackles.

Eron and Corine stood side by side on the deck of the *Angry Goddess*, each collared and bound at the wrists by rope bindings tied to leashes. They wore nothing but short cotton shifts that revealed their long legs. Each had a low-cut hole for the head and an ample show of chest, and they were open on the sides exposing their hips and the sides of their breasts. Rope belts that made sure the garments stayed closed and left them looking trim and ready for sale.

Corine still had her servant's choker in place as an added value to buyers who knew its kingdom reference. The tiny shift showed her trim hips and tight belly when the wind blew the thin material. On Eron the identical article of clothing left little to the imagination, though she could tell the simple, one-piece garment was designed for just that and for easy removal regardless of her bound wrists.

James stood behind her, holding her arms at her side as they waiting for the Shebwai navy to finishing running the gang plank over to come aboard. Telorn Bevisc stood behind Corine in the same fashion, and when she glanced back at him Eron could tell that the serving girl harbored feelings for the mate, perhaps as serious as her own towards James.

A large, bearded man with a tall turban, large belly, and huge green sash was walking across to come aboard the *Goddess*, thumbing the hilt of his large sword while he walked. Eron's expression was one of broken defiance, and she lowered her lashes when the bearded Shebwai man came towards her. In truth, though frightened, Eron was anxious and slightly elated to be at her next destination. There were times still when she wondered if this plan would ever even work, yet here she was. Still, sadness threatened to grip Eronica icily, and a part of her wished to the gods she could just stay in James's arms. "Promise me something," Eron said to James under her breath.

"Anything."

"Stay clear of Kingdom waters as much as you can. Do not be sunk by those I love nor by those that we both hate." She whispered the last as the bearded man stepped onto the *Goddess's* deck at last. "Just stay alive, James. Promise me."

"I promise," he answered low.

"Captain James Jovark of the Grey Isles," The bearded man announced with a thick accent Eron had never heard before. "You are late. By rights I should take your cargo and sink you right here!"

"General Azel Tulambec," James answered haughtily. "You may be the Sultan's closest military advisor and pretty smart for what you desert hoarders call men, but you can be a pretty unsavory bastard sometimes."

The general stepped close, nearly pinning Eron between his not inconsiderable girth and the tense muscles of the captain behind her. The Shebwai general smelled sickly-sweet, a mixture of body odor and strange incense wafting off of his beard to mix with the sour foods still caught on his breath. His clothes were made of fine silks stained at the pits and chest by copious amounts of sweat.

"You think me blind, kingdom man?" Locking hateful gaze with James over Eron's head, the general's proximity nearly crushed her. He didn't even bother to look down at her when reached out with his meaty hands and grasped Eron's breasts through the thin fabric of her shift. Eron gasped and held back a scream of pain as his fingers found her nipples and squeezed. "I see your tribute to the Sultan, scum, but it does not sway me. In another hour I would have sent forth ships to sink you and sent word to have your families in the Isles slaughtered like lambs. You're lucky I don't kill you and your pretty little slaves right here."

Eron held her breath as tears came unbidden to her eyes. She tried desperately not to twist away and gritted her teeth as her back involuntarily started to arch. At last the general released her smarting breasts and she gasped, stepping back against James.

The general glanced down at her appraisingly before returning his hateful stare to the captain. "Whatever she has been to you while you have lingered on the sea an extra day, Jovark, you can be sure that she is mine now. Perhaps I will take her to the block, or to the sultan, or perhaps I will keep her for myself. You can do nothing, kingdom scum, except hope I do not take your ship and your family's lives."

"Azel, you stinking desert rat," James said in his harshest pirate demeanor, "take your booty and search the damn ship already. I'll not sit here and trade insults with you every fucking time I sail into this damnable port." He said it simply, but James's grip on Eron's arms was like a vice. It was probably pent up anger and the desire to say even more or challenge the fat general, but Eron secretly hoped it might also be a silenced possessiveness for her.

"Search the ship," Azel commanded the soldiers coming aboard. "Report anything changed from the last time, any missing crewmen, and all booty found."

"You'll find some missing crew and my quarters ripped off of the ship," James told him before the general could move off. "We were attacked at sea by a Grahrk. It nearly sank us. That is why we are late and why I have a great bloody hole in my ship, not that you would have noticed."

General Azel Tulambec smiled, but there was nothing friendly in the gesture. "Good. Then you'll be putting in for repairs, giving us more time to search your vessel," he threatened, adding, "*captain*." The large man moved away, beginning his assessment.

"I hate that man," James seethed under his breath.

"Aye," Telorn agreed.

"Aye," Eron echoed, resisting the urge to rub her chest.

James sighed. Realizing it was their last seconds together, Eron looked up at her former captor. "You'll be fine," he reassured them both. "He'll not keep you for himself; he can't. The Sultan's rule here is absolute. Truth is, while you'll go on the block with Corine, you're probably guaranteed a position in the Sultan's own harem."

Telorn agreed quietly. "Though I've never seen the general so taken with a woman before."

"I'm glad I could impress," Eron replied.

"Return the promise, Eron," James said as two guards dressed in desert garb stepped up to take the slaves away. When they took hold of Eron and Corine's tethers to lead them away by their bound wrists, she looked back at the captain he was watching her be led away, his big brown eyes never looking sadder despite the resolute folding of his arms or the hard lines of his jaw.

Eron truly wondered if she would ever see him again.

We're to be towed into harbor, J.J.," Telorn said with an air of uncertainty.

James nodded. "I know. That snake Azel will claim it's to have us all hanged, but it's to affect repairs to the *Goddess*, be sure."

"I wish I had your confidence," the mate replied.

"Not everyone can be me, 'tis true. You just have to know how these bastards think and work," James said with a shrug. "How else do you think I made the deal that stuck us with this charge in the first place?"

"Aye," Telorn nodded with a sardonic smile, "and thanks for that."

"Better that than dead," he said to his mate, clapping him on the back. "Hope, Mr. Bevisc."

"Aye," Telorn said with a shake of his matted locks. "If you say so, cap'n."

James took Jack Kloot's magician's spyglass from the inside pocket of his coat. When no one was looking—not even those Shebwai thugs searching his deck and below—he brought the scope to his eye. The vision that greeted him surprised even James with its instant closeness and clarity. Eron's face came into view from across the waves. The wind rustled her hair as she looked across the bay, away from her escort as she was carried towards land. Her shoulders were slumped in supplication and her gaze was averted, but that same proud demeanor that had defied him was evident in Eron's brow and dark eyes. James smiled, knowing somehow that whatever master awaited her would get more than he bargained for.

Lowering the glass James tried desperately to turn his thoughts away from the girl. He watched his ship get searched for a time, shrugging off the accepted event and its simple outcomes. The crew from the Grey Isles was smart, never hiding any of their loot from the Shebwai authorities for fear of reprisal. Soon the search crew would leave and the *Goddess* would be repaired and it would be back to the sea, and somehow that made the captain smile. Looking back at the ship carrying his former cargo deep into the harbor, James wondered at the all-too-brief cause of the raise in his spirits, and hoped that she would fare well despite the nightmare he had just delivered her unto.

Chapter 8

It wasn't a crowd that congregated before the slave block of Shebwai, but a mob. Eron could scarcely believe that she would be degradingly sold in front of that sea of hungry, dirty men. "Gods, Eron," she heard Corine say, echoing her own thoughts. "What level of hell have we been admitted to?"

The market was a huge square fashioned from marble and tile in ages past, built just outside the entrance to the Port of Shebwai to make sales of newly arrived slaves quicker. The general's men had taken the two women aboard a small skiff after herding them off the deck of the *Goddess*, holding their slight shoulders in tight, unyielding grips. The short trip from the entrance of the harbor inland had taken them past naval frigates and fisherman's boats, and then along much of the seaside of the great city of Shebwai.

It afforded the girls a wondrous view of one side of the ancient city as their boat had passed. Crumbling walls in varying states of disrepair gave way to glittering, newly cleaned gateways and buildings where the more powerful and rich still dwelt as their ancestors had before them. The homes were the same, with a poor quarter that resided near the multi-leveled estates that lined the streets leading to the far-off palace. The Sultan's lair was a shining group of spires and gold-trimmed lattices that rose above it all, though the sun was behind the building, making it hard to take in at this distance. Eron gasped at its grandeur, though the castles of Capriana were scarcely larger.

All the while the general had sat next to where the bound girls watched their destination hone into view, gloating and glowering as he told them of their new home. "The Sultan entertains his slaves there," he said, pointing to the palace. "All within the land and the city of Shebwai pay him homage, as you must," he said, adding to Eron, "perhaps personally."

The skiff turned into an inlet, and more of the city was splayed out on each bank before them. "Beyond the city is the River of Life," he intoned, motioning to the inlet, "the only one of its kind for hundreds of miles.

Beyond the city and the river is nothing." When Eron kept her bowed head silent, resisting the urge to follow his baited statement with the obvious question, General Azel continued with a wry smile. "Nothing. Vast deserts surround Shebwai, making escape impossible except for either its port or by large caravans that wind into a wasteland where bandits rule with even crueler fists than that of my masters' or me. Does that frighten you, slave?" Again, Eron said nothing, content to play this new game until its next stage.

Azel grabbed Eron's hips and pulled her to his lap anyway, squeezing her waist tightly while again pinching her breast. She tried not to wince, but the general would not be satisfied until he saw pain in her eyes. "I asked you a question. A woman answers when a man speaks in my country, kingdom bitch—or she suffers punishment." He kneaded her breasts through her thin slave's shift, causing her to involuntarily squirm in his grip.

"Yes, master," Eron had finally answered to appease him.

"Master," he laughed in that thick Shebwai accent of a desert mongrel. "Jovark taught you that, did he not? Hmm?" He released her breasts and slid his hands up her barely-clothed legs. "Did he entertain you? Did he make you his own for the duration of your stay?" He released her at last, and Eron stumbled back to where Corine stood watching the scene from beneath lowered lashes. "He is no man if he did not. Had I the time I would take you here and now. But I have a job to do, and your beauty would be missed, even for an hour. Well, whatever that pirate may have done to you it is nothing compared to what awaits you in my land, slave. Of that, you can both be certain." He laughed heartily and moved away, leaving the women to their thoughts as the skiff docked at a pier at last.

Taken bodily from the small boat, Eron and Corine found themselves within a hot, clay-drab building just outside the port, handed over to the men who waited there. The general and his soldiers laughed and turned away, leaving the women to whatever new fate these sweaty dogs had in store. Soon they were being inspected by leather-clad men with slave-whips who denoted their initial price for the block after feeling up nearly each inch of their already aching bodies. The indignities suffered over those hours since leaving the *Goddess* were nothing, Eron knew, to what would come next.

"This one is exquisite," a slaver said when it came time for Eron's inspection. "We will save her for the prime slot in the roster today. Already there will be whispers about her if I know the general's tastes," he laughed.

For the briefest moment of pride, Eron smiled inwardly. It was one thing to think one's self beautiful, and more to use that asset in a mission such as hers. It was another thing entirely to have such ideals confirmed and such an ego stroked. Besides, it made Eron hopeful that the plans she and her king had made would not be in vain after all.

The slaver produced a chart and quill. "Name your place of origin and education or skills," he commanded.

Eron's voice sounded strange to her own ears as she told the filthy flesh peddler her background. "We are both from Capriana, trained at the *Chateau of Chains.*"

Impressed, the slaver bit his lip. "She goes alone," he announced, leering at Eron's body.

"No!" Eron dared haughtily. "She goes where I go."

The slaver laughed and walked up to Eron. "So commanding. Perhaps I was wrong—perhaps I should spend a few days stripping you of that Kingdom arrogance before I sell you on the block."

"You would not dare," Eron said, not nearly as certain as she sounded.

"No?" The slaver looked back at the crowd and the men talking amongst themselves as they waiting in the throng, trying to see back at the stock. "Perhaps not," he admitted. "Though I *would* dare to extend that threat to your friend here if it means controlling you."

Eron looked down, having found the limit of her power in this place. "That won't be necessary," she acquiesced. As much as she wanted to spare Corine further torture, she also did not want to miss the soonest chance to be noticed by the Sultan's possible buyers. Perhaps, if she were lucky, the same party would buy them both.

Soon the market loomed before them. Eron and Corine stood in a short line of girls of varying age and color, all dressed similarly. They were following the slave master to the edge of a stage that looked down on the market square where literally thousands of robed and shrouded men waited to bid on their flesh. Around the edges of the throng awaited several litters and carriages, some of which were richly decorated. Eron had but a moment to wonder if the Sultan himself might be among them before her attention was called to the first girl to be sold.

The lithe blonde that the block auctioneer brought forward to the crowd was a beautiful girl of perhaps nineteen. She was probably from the Isles, given her skin's sun-tanned glow, and her cheeks were stained with her tears even though she kept silent. The auctioneer held aloft a lock of her hair, igniting a roar of praise from the crowd as the bidding began. Eron and Corine watched in horror, knowing this was an example of their own selling to come.

When the bidding continued to be lower than expected for such an unbroken specimen, a large, bare-chested man standing beside the auctioneer took away the girl's rope belt and lifted her skimpy clothing over her head to reveal her nudity to the crowd. Again a cheer went up at the spectacle, and the bidding re-commenced with earnest and added value.

"Barbaric," Corine whispered. "My Lady, what are we to do?"

"We are to be sold," Eron answered coldly. She had to steal herself against what was coming, not give in to the desperation in her friend's voice and crack at the moment she must remain most proud. "Be a servant, Corine. Remember your training and do as you are bid, but do it as a Kingdom woman, not the slave they would call you."

"I cannot."

"You can," Eron nodded solemnly. "I have faith in you."

"No. I cannot be separated from you," Corine nearly sobbed.

"Perhaps we will be and perhaps not." Eron thought about how quickly events were getting out of the control she had somehow planned against weeks before while still on dry land. Once more, things were becoming complicated. "I plan to end up at the Sultan's side," she instructed, "in his harem or as a servant, whether I am bought by his men this day or not. One way or the other, if we are separated, somehow you must seek me out at the Sultan's palace or outside its walls. And be strong, Corine."

Rough hands came to the line and pulled Corine out to march her before the crowd of leering, money-waving men. "Be strong!" Eron repeated, then watched as the bidding for her servant and friend began.

"What would you give for such beauty?" the auctioneer pitched. "Young and ripe, and from the First Kingdom of Capriana itself! She has been trained at the famed *Chateau of Chains* to be a submissive in all acts of sexuality and a proper house-servant. I start the bidding for this slave at two-thousand dostinaris!" The crowd erupted into feverish bidding, with Corine left standing as a lamb to their slaughter.

"Twenty-one hundred!"

"Twenty-two hundred!"

"Bah!" the auctioneer complained, waving away the low bids. "You can do better than that!" He pulled the cowing Corine to him by her waist, undoing her rope belt and tossing it to the crowd. Turning the trembling girl around, he lifted the back of garment showing the bidders her behind. "Look at these lines! She is fit, fine, and clean. Those of you who like them lithe as well as pretty, there has been few finer than this specimen. And then there is her ability to cum on command!" He removed the Spartan cloth from over Corine's head and turned her back around to the delight of the throng. She stood nude before them, her eyes darting from the men who seemed ready to surge upon the stage and the auctioneer's guards, leering just as openly at her frail and naked body. Corine tried to bring her bound wrists to her breasts to cover them, but the auctioneer grabbed the bonds and dragged her closer to the bidders.

"Three thousand!"

"Three thousand and four!"

"Thirty-five!"

Eron closed her eyes and took a long breath, trying to calm herself. The site was the most barbaric expose' she had ever witnessed. That she would be next horrified her and made her nervous to the point of shaking knees, yet all the while it fascinated and stimulated her. She was a slave now, to be sold to the highest bidder and done with as men pleased. Corine looked so young and beautiful out there, like the finest doe ready to bolt at any moment from the surrounding stags, only to be hunted down and pinned and taken. Eron resisted the urge to let her hands creep to her throat or breasts. Instead she averted her gaze, only to have the guard nearest grip her chin to turn her eyes back to the spectacle. The giant desert man rumbled a low laugh as he watched her behold the oncoming fate.

"Forty-five," the auctioneer echoed of the highest bid thus far. "Do I hear five thousand? Going once…"

"Five thousand," a voice called.

For a moment Eron thought that the Sultan of Shebwai himself had stepped to the forefront of the throng of men. He was opulently dressed and had an air of confidence and arrogance. His turban was made of shining silks that matched his girdle, and his arms were crossed over a broad chest and swelling middle, though his face was lean and not unattractive. He stepped to the front of the stage, looking at Corine with a masked expression that was of practiced incredulity, marking the serving girl as His.

"Ah!" the auctioneer smiled with satisfaction, knowing that the bidding was over. "The Marjah bids five-thousand dostinaris. Going once. Twice. Sold, for five-thousand dostinaris to Marjah Sahbul Toremmal!"

The *Marjah*, or 'Lord' as Eron had come to understand the term, reached out to take Corine by the arm as she was led naked and barefoot to the steps from the stage. A richly dressed servant wrapped a cloak around her body, and just before she was led away to a waiting litter, Corine looked back fearfully at her mistress. She tried to give a weak smile, but the thin curtains of the litter that bore her away eclipsed her face.

Corine was gone.

"Next!"

Eron was brought forward to the center of the stage, where the auctioneer himself all but groped and fondled her while drinking in her visage with his slavering eyes. The crowd surged forward to get a better look, for while a brunette was hardly a rare commodity in this land, Eron's pale skin and beauty were obviously of uncommon equal. She stepped back, only to have a guard lock his meaty hands on her shoulders with a bruising grip. She felt the tall man close behind her, his hardening manhood evident through thin silks against her own nearly bare bottom.

"A truly rare commodity, my friends," the auctioneer said, and the din of voices quieted to hear what this new offering had in store for them. "The blonde was but an appetizer before her mistress; a Lady of the First Kingdom, trained in the same *Chateau* as her servant and one of the finest fillies I have ever laid eyes on. Her sexuality and pedigree are without question, with a flawless body and red, ripe lips unparalleled for kissing—or for other ventures!" The crowd laughed and jeered at the innuendo, looking at each other and then at Eron. Hundreds of eyes all ready to devour her, hands ready to drag her down, to rend her clothes asunder and take her over and over. Eron fought hard to breathe without looking frightened for her life. "I start the bidding at five-thousand dostinaris!"

The crowd roared with bids or rage, some willing to try for the beauty standing scantily clad before them, others having nowhere near the money needed for such a purchase.

"Hold!" a voice called, cutting the noise of the crowd to a whisper in an instant. Eron looked to the voice, finding another man dressed richly like the Marjah, though his cloaks and sashes were uniform with another man standing near the same litter and its bearers. Also standing next to the new voice was general Azel, looking directly at her. He had said that Eron was to be the Sultan's if not his, so she could only hope that the men and the litter all belonged to the most powerful man in Shebwai.

The elegant figure stepped up to the stage and mounted the steps, holding out a bound scroll and a bag of clinking money to the auctioneer. To his credit, the slave-master ignored the money, simply bowing and stepping aside for the servant to inspect Eron firsthand.

The man was handsome and tall, his dark skin and style markedly different from any other that she had ever been this close to. Eron forgot to avert her eyes from his when he stepped up to her and began to finger her hair and look over her body. His hands were strangely soft and hot, Eron noticed, when they reached out to feel her skin. "We will take her," the man said, and threw the bag of gold to the auctioneer.

Without even checking the amount in the leather purse handed to him, the slaver bowed again and waved her away. "With blessings, sir," he said, and waved to the guard to take her away with this man.

The crowd was silent as Eron was cloaked by the soft-handed servant and led from the stage and through the throng of hot, teeming men to where the general and the glittering litter waited. She could still only assume that the Sultan was behind its rich curtains, and that it was his power and not the general's that commanded such quiet acquiescence of the prematurely ended auction of her flesh. Eron held her breath and stepped into the waiting mobile pavilion, keeping her head bowed when she passed the chuckling general.

"Get in, slave," general Azel said with a motion of his hand. Eron did as she was ordered, parting the curtain to find an empty, cushioned bed within. She had but a moment to stare in surprise at the vacant space before the general stepped up behind her and seized Eron's shoulders. "You are lucky, kingdom bitch." One hand held her shoulder while another made a sweeping gesture that traveled down the length of her arched spine, cupping one buttock beneath her short garb briefly before reaching around to grasp and knead her plump breasts. "Lucky that I am loyal to the Sultan. Lucky that I know my place within his land and that he gives me servants of my own to break. He may keep the best for himself, but it is still my job to point them out for a man who never leaves his palace walls."

His cruel hands continued to squeeze her flesh through the thin material of her short shift, venturing down the front neckline to further his molestations. Eron simply stood there in wide-eyed shock, uncertain of what he was going to do. Was he keeping her for himself, to take to his own palace and 'break'?

"Enough, general," came the voice of the soft-handed servant. Azel's hands froze where they lay, still clamped like steel sweat to Eron's skin beneath her shift. She held her breath, desperate not to be reduced to a panicked, panting victim in his stiff grip, even as her own betraying nipples hardened against his palm. "You've made your point, and the Sultan thanks you for letting us know of this particular prize. Now leave her be—the divan is for her travel to the master, not your brand of sport."

Azel's hands slid out from beneath Eron's slave garb. "Just extracting my toll for the find, Mahlek," the giant bearded general grinned. He slapped her ass, nearly sending her sprawling onto the cushions with the force of the blow. "I'll be thinking of you when I fuck my own kingdom whore this night," Azel laughed at her.

"'Tis done, Azel. She is my charge now." His tone became harder. "You're tribute is noted, whether I needed you or not. Now hands off, and go about your own business and leave me to mine."

General Azel shook his head at the handsome servant and began to depart. "You must be castrated, Mahlek. How can you not tumble each one of these fillies before you take them to His Holiness? If I were you, I'd be…"

"I'm aware of your appetites," Mahlek challenged. "The Sultan thanks us *both* for our loyalty."

Azel laughed, but finally departed.

"Be seated," Mahlek gestured to the cushions. "The Harem awaits."

"The Sultan's Harem?" Eron ventured, still uncertain of her destination.

"His Holiness, the Sultan of Shebwai, has purchased you for his personal Harem," the servant said evenly. "This litter shall carry us to that place of honor, where you are destined to spend the rest of your life caring for His needs."

'Bearing his children and cooking his meals, I suppose?' Eron wanted to throw at him, but she held back. She was here for a purpose, and for that she had an act to play. Bowing her head, the former Lady Eronica of Tibeth climbed into the litter and pulled her long legs under herself, making room for the Sultan's servant as he climbed aboard as well. Mahlek sat with his legs crossed, situating and composing himself before snapping his fingers to the litter-bearers without. A metal decanter of the strange, swirling desert design was handed to him, and he drank heartily of the water within before handing it to Eron. When he snapped his fingers again, the curtains were closed and Eron had to work to keep from spilling the offered water when the slaves raised the litter. She quickly got used to the odd sensation of human-born motion, and silently Eron rode the final leg of her journey to the palace of the Sultan of Shebwai.

What is your name?" Mahlek asked, breaking the silence as the gates opened to the Sultan's luscious palace. The slaves picked the litter up once more and trotted the length of paved road winding up a garden path.

"Eronica," Eron said, never taking her eyes off of her rich new surroundings. "I am called Eron." She tried to sound scared or submissive, but she was too busy being fascinated by the alien flora and architecture of the grounds and the looming castle beyond. Men and women of varying age and description toiled under the hot sun, but the shade of the trees and smaller structures made their work look like the ease of gardening paradise itself. The brown, dusty surroundings of the city made Eron appreciate the scale and spectacle of the palace grounds even more so.

Suddenly they were under a giant, gilded overhang adjacent to the main building, where several other empty litters waited with slaves and servants. Eron's transport was lowered, and Mahlek exited the curtains, taking her hand to help her out as well.

"Bring Laurallin," he commanded a tall woman of olive complexion. The woman turned and ran into the palace, and Eron watched her depart, taking the moment to study her and the others that had greeted the arrival of Mahlek's litter. Again she found that the age groups ran the full range from childhood to senior, and their skin colors varied as well. Most were the brown or olive of desert dwellers, though some were even darker, while a few were lighter skinned, as though from perhaps one of the Five Kingdoms or southern principality. Their garb also depended on their function. Slaves and creatures of simple designation or beauty were dressed in very little at all, though again the fabrics were of rich weave. Litter-bearers and other officials, on the other hand, were covered from head to toe in robes, turbans, sashes, and laces. Armed guards holding ornate pikes stood by the gates and doors, and Eron could see their piercing gaze caressing her from beneath each veiled helm.

For an instant, thoughts of Corine and what her new surroundings might be like clouded Eron's mind.

The olive-skinned servant returned, followed by a woman of rare poise and attractiveness, dressed only in a clingy sash about her shapely hips and thin golden-hued gauze that barely concealed her full breasts. She was in her late thirties, Eron surmised, and striking—with long black hair and sun-darkened skin. But her features held a cold beauty; her arched, thin eyebrows the only curve to her even and masked face that regarded Eron as though she were nothing. "Yes?" she asked of Mahlek, her accented tongue just as tempered and calculating as her expression.

Mahlek ignored her demeanor. "This is Eron, formerly of the Kingdom of Capriana, where she was a Lady. She was purchased at the Auction today for His Holiness's harem." Turning to Eron, he told her, "Laurallin is the Sultan's favorite, and therefore elevated to the position of Harem Overseer."

Laurallin seemed to notice her for the first time, running her eyes up and down the length of Eron's body with a look nearing disapproval. "Well done, Mahlek. She's almost pretty." Again Eron had to hold her temper in check, instantly wishing to lash out with more than words for such a jealous insult to her looks and title. Instead she glared for only a moment before lowering her long lashes in submission. "Come along," Laurallin continued with an air of boredom. "Let's get you cleaned up."

Eron glanced once more at the guards and slaves surrounding her, wondering if she would ever be able to escape this strange new world she'd gotten herself into.

The harem was an entire wing of the palace, it seemed. Long halls and large rooms, all decorated with planted vases, gorgeous decorated cushions and rugs, and intricate latticework met Eron's suddenly hungry eyes. Her wrists were still bound in front of her dust-covered slave's shift. Eron swallowed her remaining pride and tried not to feel humiliated as she was led down the halls in front of so many other pretty girls.

"This is your new home," Laurallin announced haughtily. "Grander, I'm sure than any house of wood or brick in your lands, *Lady*."

Women aged from late teens to early forties lingered in archways or peeked from behind screens to watch the new girl being led through her new lodgings. Some giggled and whispered to their roommates, while others scowled or shook their heads in sadness at the spectacle, fingering fresh collars about their own necks. All were near-perfect specimens of beauty, wrapped in golden chains and threads of silver or amber, many topless. A few were fair-haired, and there were even a small number of redheads, again reminding Eron of Corine's unknown plight.

"In here," Laurallin said, leading her into a vast tiled chamber. "The Bathhouse, "she said, and clapped her hands so that some of the youngest girls nearby came running to do their mistress's bidding. "You will come here of your own accord whenever you are not fresh. His Holiness may call on any one of us at any time, and you must be ready."

The room instantly harkened Eron's memory of the sauna rooms of the *Chateau*, though mostly it was simply large steam rooms, pools, and tiled floors for bathing in tubs or hot showers. There were a few large iron-looking rings set into the wall here and there that might be used for binding a person, but Eron wasn't given time to wonder or study. Instead she was hastened into an adjacent room that was open to the pool and showers but fitted with a beautiful marble vanity and seat.

Freeing her bonds, Laurallin again regarded Eron's current dusty wear with disdain. "Strip, girl. The Sultan will not receive you in those rags, smelling of a slaver's ship or paltry Kingdom perfumes." Three girls that had followed at Laurallin's command giggled at the prodding their mistress handed out, but stayed otherwise silent. Eron did as she had been told, briefly dispensing with her captive demeanor to proudly throw off the rope belt and dirty shift, revealing her stunning, if somewhat disheveled, body to her new comrades. The giggles stopped, and for a moment the girls regarded her perfect form in all of its splendor, standing sweaty yet proud before them.

When she regarded Laurallin with knowing eyes, Eron again saw a barely concealed jealousy smoldering there. This woman was to be her rival, Eron knew. If she was to work her way through the ranks of the harem to be near the Sultan when it was most important, than Laurallin was the one to topple or impress, depending on what might be necessary as the days ahead came to hopeful fruition.

The Harem's Overseer waved for the girls to take her away. "Shower the filth of the city from her," she commanded. "Bring her back here quickly so that we may make her presentable."

Before Eron could be taken away, Laurallin grasped chin and stared into her defiant eyes. "No questions? No begging or tears? You're stronger than most, girl, I'll give you that." Then she added ominously; "Or more than you seem." She turned away from the new slave and began preparing body paints and other items, saying, "This is where you live and die from this day forward. Get used to it, 'Eron'. It is a cage, but it is a gilded one, for certain. When you are not performing *whatever* the Master tells you to do, you can relax here with the others amongst the splendor and comfort of the harem. Or you can make enemies and be defiant and tossed aside as sport by myself or the Sultan for it—your choice."

Eron said nothing, but followed the other strangely quiet girls towards the showers and steam rooms, thankful to be bathed at last.

Chapter 9

This is going to take some time," the foreman said. The spindly little Shebwai man, old but spry and experienced, was standing next to James. Both were staring at the rear of the *Angry Goddess* as it was being tethered. He wiped his brow and bare chest with a filthy rag, then pointed at the gaping hole the sea Grahrk had torn out of the vessel. "I'll do what I can, but Kingdom design isn't my strong suit. She'll look at little different, but she'll be as sea-worthy as ever."

Captain James Jovark raised an eyebrow at the prospects and then accepted his fate. "Do what you can, Azim."

"Who's paying for this, anyway?"

It was as good a question as any James had heard in some time. "If the Sultan or the general doesn't cover it, I've been allotted enough in the past year to repair my own mistakes, I'm sure," he answered dryly.

Azim waved away the privateer's name-dropping but said, "I'll have my men get right on it, Northerner."

Telorn Bevisc was sitting nearby, lighting a long pipe. "Shore leave, J.J.?"

"I don't want to be here," James grumbled. "But we've no choice." The city and the hold it had on James and his crew hung thick in the air for him. He didn't like the people who inhabited it nor the disdain they had for Kingdom men, and the military presence and its build-up was even worse. It all offered too many possibilities for tempers to get out of hand, including his own.

And then there was Eron. Lost somewhere within the vast cityscape of Shebwai, she was in even worse captivity than James's own outlook. Being stuck here with her so near and yet so completely out of reach was strangely maddening; it left her on his mind in a new unsettling sort of way that kept her face wrapped around the tip of his mind. He could no more escape her while trapped in Shebwai than Eron could escape whatever prison she had been led to. The same emotions that had helped start his day with a renewed sense of hope and self were now drowned by longing. James hadn't known such feelings since being captured and exiled from the Grey Isles.

He sighed, trying to put such ideas out of his mentality. "We'll confine the bulk of the crew to the ship to hasten repairs. Small groups can go ashore for short periods—anything we can do keep anyone from being arrested or killed. They cut off limbs and tongues for transgressions in this backward hellhole, and I'll give up no more blood to Shebwai 'justice.'"

"Understood, cap'n," Telorn nodded, handing the lit pipe to his friend.

James took a long drag of the sweet tobacco, expelling the smoke from the corner of his mouth. He looked up at the hot sun and wheeling birds, hoping night would fall soon.

"So," Telorn began with a smile, "What was she like?"

Thoughts of the past days reeled through James's mind again. He wanted to answer with the passion he felt at the memories. He wanted to say that she had been beautiful, amazing, tender, soft, alluring, gorgeous— anything to give real meaning to the way Eron had made James felt. All he could answer, though, staring at the searing sky was; "hotter than the sun."

"Think she ended up bought by the Sultan?"

"Probably." James tried not to think about it. "The real question is whether the other girl ended up with her."

"Corine?" Telorn shrugged.

"I knew it. You're taken with her."

"Hey, she's a beautiful girl," the first mate answered without apology. "Besides, the things she can do with her lips… It makes me want to compose songs." He lowered his voice and glanced about him conspiratorially. "I've half a mind to find her and steal her away with us when we leave this city if I thought no one would ever know who took her."

James couldn't say aloud the fact that similar ideas had sprung briefly to him. "Set the crew to work and compose the first shore group of six men," he ordered instead, handing the wooden pipe back.

"Aye," Telorn stood. "I'll remind them of the penalties of Sultan law before I release them on the city."

"You do that," James agreed, his thoughts becoming dark, like Eron's hair.

Am I to meet the Sultan tonight?" Eron asked Laurallin when she returned. After the silence among these strangers, the conversation was welcome, regardless of whom it was.

The three girls Laurallin commanded continued primping Eron with practiced skill and zeal. The shower had not lacked eroticism, with its three naked bodies scrubbing her own pure of the rigors of travel. Ultimately it had been a simple cleaning, though, and Eron had been hurried back to where the vanity and new clothes awaited her. Her hair was brushed dry and left in flattering waves and her nails trimmed and filed before being coated in a glittering polish. She still sat otherwise nude before the mirror as the group attended her.

"You are to begin your servitude to His Holiness," Laurallin answered curtly. "You will be in his presence and presented to him, but whether that means he will ignore you, fuck you, or have me beat you will depend on his whim, and his alone. That is what it means to be new here."

Submission was something she would grant her new master, the Sultan. This bitch, however, was already getting on Eron's nerves. "How long before I can have your job?"

The girl brushing Eron's hair froze mid-stroke, and the others stiffened as well, not having heard that sort of defiance from a new girl anytime recently. It was a calculated risk, she knew, but Eron figured any recriminations would have to wait until after her presentment.

Laurallin, on the other hand, actually laughed a little, though her mouth was set firm in a hard, thin smile. "No time soon with that attitude, little slave." She leaned over Eron's shoulder to speak directly into her ear. "The other girls hate me, Eron, because while any one of them may pleasure the Sultan if he wishes it, only I have his ear." She pulled on Eron's hair, causing the Kingdom woman to wince. "But perhaps you're right. Perhaps I should *announce* the 'Lady' of the Kingdom. That way I'm sure that the

Sultan will have something special planned for you by the time you're ready." She released Eron and looked at the other girls who could not meet her cruel gaze the way Eron had. "Make her look perfect. Use the body powders and perfumes after you've shaved that repugnant Kingdom fashion from between her legs."

Laurallin stormed off, and the three girls released a collective sigh of thankfulness.

"You shouldn't talk to her like that," one said.

"Yeah, you're in for it now," another added.

"I can take it," Eron snorted. "Anything to wipe the smugness away for a moment."

The third girl harrumphed at that, but set back to work on Eron's hair. "You say that now, but Laurallin really does have the Sultan's ear. If she wants one or all of us punished in front of the entire court for amusement, he'll do it for her. Gods know why—she's hardly the best lay around here anymore—at her age."

"Yeah," the first agreed with a subdued laugh. "I'm pretty sure he's been spending more time with Sacha of late than any of us, perhaps even more so than Laurallin. But that hasn't stopped the Harem Mistress from having Sacha flogged at the Sultan's feet simply because it was a night's diversion."

"True," the one combing Eron's hair agreed, nodding to her. "Sacha's an outlander, like you. Maybe that's why Laurallin doesn't like you—jealous of His Holiness's preoccupation with girls from conquered lands of late."

The others waved that away. "If she's jealous it's because this one's beautiful."

"Thank you," Eron said, relaxing a little. "What's your name?"

"Embeth. That's Zatahlia and Ula brushing your hair."

"Hello."

"Greetings," Ula answered. "Don't let your guard down too much at first, Eron. There's a hierarchy around here, for certain, and Laurallin's at the top. Embeth's right—I think you're already on the menu tonight."

"Are you really…" Eron looked down at her small nest of brown curls. "Do you really have to shave me?"

"Of course," Embeth answered, turning Eron around getting a razor and some soap. "'Tis customary in Shebwai, and clean."

"Oh. I see," Eron answered nervously. She watched as the slave girl rinsed her lower extremities down again briefly before applying soap, and finally setting to work with the razor's blade. Within moments the hair was shorn away by the dangerous looking knife and the moment was passed. Eron looked down to find her body bare and her cleft clearly visible, leaving her feeling more naked than she had in a long time. Now she wasn't so sure she was ready to be thrust into whatever the evening had in store for her.

Eron was led into the room like a sacrifice. Two men held her by the arms as she was marched forward into the vast throne room where a hundred desert courtesans waited to see the Sultan's new toy.

She was clad in a diaphones skirt that was riding below her supple hips and open all the way to the top of one leg. The nearly-transparent fabric was attached to a tiny set of bottoms so low cut in the front that had she not been shorn her pubic hair would certainly have been showing, and the garment's back was equally scandalous. A small half-bodice fell from her round shoulders and strained to keep from spilling Eron's magnificent breasts out for all to see. Gold and jewels, the likes of which Eron had never been able to afford even while in the employ of the King himself, adorned her ears and neck. Bangles jingled above brass shackles on her wrists connected by a thin golden chain that matched the one around her waist.

A strap of black leather, like a thin choker with a ring set in it for leashing, adorned her throat marking her as a slave of the palace. The others were near-nude, male and female each, and while some carried platters of food or drink. Some were chained to walls or their masters, and a select few were tethered to the Sultan's throne itself. The assembled patrons, in comparison, were wearing strange gowns and jackets with billowing pants made of superb tapestries or sashes and robes of silk. Eron knew that future evenings would be less dramatic. This was a public claiming—a presentation of new flesh before a God:

The pomp and circumstance of her first night in the Sultan's Harem.

The Sultan, a far-off figure seated on a throne of marble and gold, waved Eron's escorts forward. Her hands clasped uneasily behind her arched back as she was nearly dragged by the giant guards at her sides.

"Beautiful," and "Stunning" were the few words in her own tongue that Eron could make out as she was led past the throng. Their sharp intakes of breath and appreciative eyes gave Eron a strength that might have otherwise been lacking. Where Eron had once been the rich courtesan gazing upon a royal spectacle, she was now the chained entertainment for the evening. A spring began to wind in the pit of her stomach, making her knees momentarily give way.

The Sultan's voice snapped Eron back into reality. "Let us see our pleasure."

As Eron approached she finally got her first look at the mysterious man of her childhood dreams and nightmares. The most powerful and dangerous man in the world south of the Kingdoms sat erect in his seat, his face a dark brown vision of strength. High cheekbones and a tall forehead would have given him chiseled features if his unlined face hadn't been so rounded. Eron couldn't tell if the Sultan of Shebwai was thirty years old or fifty, but from what she understood he was nearing middle age. He hardly seemed it. His expansive shoulders and broad chest denoted physical perfection under those silks and sashes, while his wide, bright eyes shone with scary intensity from beneath black brows and a dark turban of blue. The sultan's ringed fingers waved again—*closer.*

Behind the slaves grouped around the Sultan's throne stood a black man in an equally dark cloak, his face somewhat hidden beneath a hood. His featureless garb did nothing to hide the power that resided within this figure. Not only was his physique massive, but an aura all but emanated from this man. This, and the belt of pouches and potions on his belt, led Eron to believe that this was the Sultan's personal necromancer—the wizard rumored to be much of the true power behind the Sultan's reign. His face was stern, with long beard extending from his meaty chin. Eron had to tear her eyes away from his piercing gaze that somehow threatened to discover her secrets. She lowered her own long lashes rather than be forced to instead match the Sultan's scrutiny.

At the Sultan's side, standing free and unchained aside from her collar, was Laurallin. She was dressed similarly to Eron, only she stood proudly, with a smirk on her lips that suggested she was enjoying what was about to happen. "Your pleasure, Holiness," She said.

Holding up his hand to silence the jeering crowd of revelers, the Sultan smiled and leaned forward to see his new pet better. "What sport have you provided this evening, Laurallin?" came his thick accent. He stood, taking a long strand of silken chord in his hand as he came to stand at the base of the steps where Eron was held. His smoldering gaze and teasing smile softened when he came to study her, and Eron, wilting in the vice-like grip of the guards raised her chin to regard him with silent defiance.

"This is Eronica, formerly of the Kingdoms, Your Holiness," Laurallin announced. "She is indicative of their race—a wildcat that must be broken as an example so that all of her kind know that your power is absolute." She held a bullwhip in her hands, and Eron almost gasped at the sight. The weapon could flay the flesh from her bones if administered with the cruel intentions the Harem Overseer implied.

The Sultan's appreciation of Eron's body lingered on her heaving chest, flat stomach and scantily clad thighs. He stroked her cheek in a way that was almost tender, though Eron knew it was simply admiration of an object of rarity. "This creature is far too beautiful for what you propose, my pet."

Laurallin's anger was barely held in check. "Master, you agreed…"

"I agreed that my new slave should be brought forth as sport this evening," he interrupted. "She certainly will be that. But not to the degree you suggest. Not tonight and not for all to see—this night she is mine." The sultan held Eron by the chin, and she could feel his hot breath caress her sweat-chilled flesh. "She will either learn to serve, as you say she cannot, or she will learn the folly of such defiance. If she displeases me, then we will do as you suggested." Before the enraged Laurallin could protest further, he looked back at her to quiet her anger. "Together, if and when it is warranted, we can take our time reducing her to nothing, and for all to see. But the only thing more delicious than destroying such an exquisite vessel of foreign defiance would be to make her my own."

He took the chord of silk and threaded it through the ring at Eron's neck, tying it in place as a lead. The guards released her arms and the Sultan of Shebwai led her up the stairs to his throne, where he sat amongst giant cushions and pulled the pliant flesh of Eron's waist to him to be seated on his lap. Laurallin glared at Eron for only a moment before returning her features to a mask of compliance for the crowd. Eron sat silently on the Sultan's thigh, marveling at both the expansive room she was showcased to, but also at the sudden turn of events that had put her in such an oddly enviable position.

"Continue," the Sultan commanded the revelers.

Music and mirth recommenced, and Eron waited where she sat while her new master stroked her skin and hair. He began to chat with his subjects as each approached, and soon the chamber was a buzz of conversation and drink. Despite her lack of knowledge regarding her current position and surroundings, Eron took the time allowed to think hard on the next stage of her plan.

Her breath froze in her throat when she spied the Marjah Sahbul Toremmal among the guests, but further questing of his entourage told Eron that Corine was not among them. Despair momentarily gripped Eron's emotions, but was put aside by sheer force of will. She was where she had promised her king she would be—on the lap of the Sultan of Shebwai, learning the inner workings of his court by being close enough to kill. She wondered who, if anyone, in the room might also be agents for the First Kingdom, and if anyone might be her eventual contact to get her back out.

She glanced only once at the enemies around her—the wizard regarding Eron with lustful suspicion and the Harem mistress with her burning daggers for eyes.

Hands still bound loosely behind her, Eron bowed her spinning head. The Sultan led her by leash into his personal chambers after the hours of revelry. She had spent the evening sitting on his lap or at the base of his throne whenever he got up to mingle. When slaves had offered wine to her she had taken it and drank in silence, and when the Sultan had whispered in her ear Eron had nodded or cowered as she felt the moment required. She was sober enough to stand in her spiked heels when he commanded and had at last led her from the chamber, promising the crowd he would test the new slave enough for all present to be satisfied.

"The Sultan is not usually interested in raping some virgin or being served by a naïve, un-spirited girl," Embeth had told her before leaving her to the evening's discourse. "Whether he demands immediate obedience or is in the mood to conquer you, he will want an experienced woman, able to please him in whatever way he commands or desires."

There was not much, if anything, that the Sultan did not command in this place. The room, like the grounds around the palace, was perfectly kept by the servants in attendance. Eron wondered if there was a private place in the whole city to find her contacts within. Two men and two women, all nude save for sarongs about their waists, stood silently in the corners, each more beautiful than the last. The chamber, immense and currently open to the stars in one portion of ceiling and walls, was carved of marble, tile, and gold. Beautiful accents and furniture adorned some of the space, and a gigantic bed upon a raised dais was at the center, covered in cushions and fanned by two more slaves. Nearby were gilded trays with perfumes, food, grapes, drinks –

And sexual toys.

Whips, crops, phalluses, ropes and other tools were arrayed for use. The corners of the bed reminded Eron of the posts and bindings in James's cabin, only instead of wood pillars and rope, golden chains and marble columns awaited the Sultan's pleasure. Eron tried not to stare with such wide-eyed intrigue and fear, but this room alone put the *Chateau De Chaines* to shame. Suddenly she felt more boxed in and totally alone and at the mercy of another than ever before in her life. Panic stole into Eron's heart, though she brushed it aside with everything she could muster, determined to win this man's lust over with equal satisfaction.

The Sultan threw his belt and sashes upon the cushions of the bed. "Welcome," he repeated. He walked back to where he had tethered her to a hook high on a bed column. "Tell me your name again," he commanded, softly stroking her cheek.

His presence, suddenly so much more intimate than having been on his lap in front of hundreds of revelers, was an intoxication that left Eron's throat dry. Perhaps it was the wine, she told herself. "Eronica, master," she answered, clenching her bound hands behind her slim back. "They call me Eron, for short."

"Eronica. I am Jatuu Olumbai, Sultan of Shebwai, Holiness of Tumquai, and Son of the God Lil. I am supreme here. You understand this?"

"Yes, master," Eron answered, watching his fingers with downward cast eyes as he traced her lips and jaw. Her breath became shallow as he lowered the familiarizing hand to her chest, knowing what was coming.

"You are a slave here. Mine to do with as I please." His voice was calm and quiet, almost soothing, and his closeness was warm and invigorating with its foreign feel and smells. His hands moved to the clasp between her breasts and deftly released it, exposing them as the tight garment popped open. "You understand this?"

Eron's chest heaved as the fear and excitement of what was about to happen all but overwhelmed her with his effortless action. This man meant to have her, here and now, and quite simply because he could. She tried to control her breathing and remain proud, nodding as she answered. "Yes, master."

His hands reached out to cup and then fondle her breasts. "Square your shoulders back," he told her when she began to slouch them into his fingers' embrace. His thumbs and forefingers began to tug and pinch her plump nipples as they became erect. "I may fuck you here and now, Eronica. I may instead command that you service me or another slave. Or ten. Do you understand this?"

Eron tossed her hair, briefly making eye contact with her new master. "Yes, master," she repeated suggestively, and leaned forward to kiss his silk-lined chest.

A slave gasped. Eron glanced over to see him step forward in preparation to restrain her from the Sultan if needed, but Jatuu held up a hand to stop him in his tracks. "Let her. She is an outlander, and does not know our ways." He looked Eron in the eyes and gave her a smile that could have been keen interest, or could have been a wolf waiting for prey to step within the trap. "Continue."

Eron knelt down in front of him, causing the leash to pull tight at the collar around her neck and her shoulders and arms to wriggle with involuntary struggle. Regardless, her lips pressed against the soft material of his trousers to seek out his hips and then his manhood. She could feel his heat through the thin cloth barring his erection from her, and she breathed an equally hot breath against it when her mouth finally found his center. Eron glanced up again, waiting for some trap to spring and his sudden declaration of heresy against her master, the Son of a God. She honestly didn't know if he would loose his prick for her to suck or call the guards in to have her beaten—or worse.

Jatuu stepped back, causing the kneeling Eron to pull at the leash, móuthing hungrily at the air where his encased cock had just been. He regarded her with a knowing grin for a moment's indecision, and then he finally removed his trousers and brought his engorged erection to her face.

Eron had but a moment to observe the Sultan's cock before she let it slide between her parted lips. The large, thick member filled the recesses of her mouth, and she wondered if this man's was larger than James's. Eron put such warm thoughts aside, concentrating instead on the task at hand. She wrapped her moist lips around her new master's manhood and began to suck gently.

Tastes and perfumes Eron had never experienced before assailed her senses. For a time she wondered if she would be able to enjoy pleasuring this man in this way, much less keep from gagging on his girth as it slid down her throat. She tried not to think of the others in the room who could see her used in this way. Regardless of social standing, she was not an exhibitionist and wished this event were a private one.

Eventually the strange qualities crowding her thoughts and psyche subsided and Eron worked breathlessly at pumping her head up and down the length of his shaft. She dared not let him slip out for fear of what it might mean, given her level of servitude. She concentrated instead on using friction and the wet confines of her mouth and teeth to entice him further.

"Lower," he commanded, and gripped his shaft to raise it over her face. She took Jatuu's lead and nestled her nose under his large balls to lick the underside of each. The position again put pressure on her constricting throat thanks to the tight leash, but Eron liked the way that heightened the already overpowering feelings of excitement and danger. It made her pussy clench and moisten and her nipples harden to an almost painful state. "Yes, there," he exclaimed, stroking himself with his large hand and making her lick the base of the shaft before placing his crotch back over her face. She took one side of his hot sack into her mouth and sucked with more force, causing Jatuu to groan aloud. Eron almost laughed, so overwrought with the emotions that came with being able to please a man that could just as easily have her thrown back to Laurallin's cruel punishments. Perhaps she was impressing the Sultan after all.

Jatuu grunted once more as her little tongue licked and teased the underside of his balls and between his thighs. When he did, his strokes brought him to orgasm and suddenly Eron's face was being showered in hot jets of white cum. He stepped back again and placed the tip of his cock on her outstretched tongue, continuing to squirt his load into her mouth and drip it onto her full breasts. Eron closed her eyes and accepted his gift, letting him finish covering her with his seed, all while his slaves looked on.

"You do this well, Eron," the Sultan said, evidently pleased. "We are at a dilemma, then, you and I: Laurallin wants you punished for some slight you gave her today. As I expect her to someday give me an heir, I do occasionally gratify her wishes. She has led me to believe that you will be a worthless slave, good only for punishment. Instead you surprise me with passion and skill."

Jatuu thought on this while he finished removing his clothes, leaving his splendid form and desert darkened skin bare to Eron's appraisal. His muscular chest and arms resembled his face—not chiseled, but round yet firm. The Sultan's belly was flat and devoid of hair, unlike James who's hardened abs and dark curls had fascinated Eron. Equally thick, powerful thighs steadied the Sultan's tall, broad frame.

"However," Jatuu continued at last, "Laurallin's age is advancing, and still she has not brought me a son. Tell me, Eron, do you think perhaps it is she that should be punished? For this, as well as for deceiving me as to your abilities?"

Eron knew the Sultan was playing with her, but was still unsure of his character. He might indeed want her to speak her mind, but more likely could at any moment have her taken away. "I'm sure I don't know, master," she dared to answer.

Jatuu looked at her with mock scrutiny. "Such prowess and forward indiscretions, but you shirk at answering me with you mind?"

"I would not presume so far that I be thrown into the dungeon, master," she answered.

Jatuu laughed genuinely. "Of course. That is wise. I will make you a deal, Eronica of the Kingdoms. In Laurallin's interest, I will punish you tonight, but in our own interests, I will do this only lightly—providing I can make you climax at least twice. You cannot fake this, for I will know whether or not you are truly reaching orgasm. And if you do not climax twice, or if I suspect you are faking, then I will have you beaten in the manner the Harem Mistress wishes."

Eron trembled at the thought of relying on climaxing multiple times in this extraordinary new place with a threatening, powerful man performing Gods-knew-what acts on her flesh as complete strangers watched.

"Do you agree?"

Chapter 10

Do you agree?" the Sultan repeated.

Eron knew that this was not a question of Jatuu's prowess or ego. As Sultan he had his pick of women to either love or leave. He was testing her; he wanted to know if Eron would allow herself to be His. He wanted her to give in totally to him and accept her position as a member of his Harem, resigned to Jatuu's ability to stimulate her and no one else's, perhaps ever again.

Eron nodded. "Yes, master."

"Stand." He brought her close to him with an arm around her thin waist, using a silken towel to wipe Eron's face at last. His fingers went to the laces of her garment still hanging by her shoulders and began to undue them. Jatuu deftly removed the garment with quick ease and tossed it onto the rug beneath them, and then his hands went to her hips. He tore the veil around her waist free with a single pull, eliciting a tiny gasp from Eron. His hungry mouth captured and suckled at one breast as his fingertips worked their way under the tight band that kept her tiny shorts on her body, tearing those free as well. Her bared and shorn mound was open to him now, and his palms briefly caressed and explored her naked skin. He towered over Eron again, smiling with satisfaction.

She looked up into Jatuu's eyes as he spoke to her. "You are beautiful, Eron. Truly one of the most beautiful women I have ever seen. It would please me to make you mine, for such beauty deserves adoration, not scars. I don't want to toss you aside, but I will if I find you unworthy." His words sounded cold and uncaring, but he spoke them so fluently and sincerely that she was drawn to the idea of pleasing him.

Jatuu's hand at the small of her back dipped between her bound wrists and down the cleft of her buttocks. He calmly massaged her there while fondling her creamy breasts with open appraisal. After another moment of caressing her form with his hands and his strangely white eyes, he reached up and untied the chord leashing Eron to the bed frame. "Lay back," he commanded at last.

Uncertain as to what her new master might be up to, but powerless to do anything else, Eron complied. She climbed onto the soft, billowing pillows and turned her body so that she was on her back. With one knee slightly raised, she arched her back, both to please him with her jutting breasts, but also to alleviate the pressure on her bound wrists underneath her. Closing her eyes for an instant, Eron took in a breath to calm her racing heart. *What is he going to do?*

"Spread your thighs," he told her.

Eron did so obediently. Opening her eyes, she watched with trepidation as Jatuu climbed onto the bed and knelt over her, his massive cock standing erect and waiting. Eron felt so naked, shaved and spread like that beneath his waiting member. In one hand the Sultan held a flogger, with a long, thick handle of wrapped leather that culminated into a ball, giving the shaft an appearance not unlike a phallus. In his other hand was a small, short chain with clips on either end.

"Hold still," he said, and opened one of the clips, placing it onto the plump nipple of her left breast.

"Ungh," she moaned involuntarily. The pressure was unrelenting and painful, but the clip stayed attached to her thick peak and somehow didn't crush it. She hissed in a breath and bit her lip at the Sultan attached the second clip to her other nipple, then ceased to breath when he tugged slightly at the chain connecting her breasts. The clips held as he pulled higher, displacing her large breasts with the motion.

Eron was still gritting her teeth when Jatuu presented her with the chain. "Open your mouth," he commanded, and placed the chain between her jaws. "Close." She did so, finding herself holding her raised breasts in their current, painful position with her own mouth. "Do not bow your head," he warned. "You must hold your bosom erect. If you release them or slacken the pull, I shall only punish you worse for it."

Eron could only whimper a response as she stared at him kneeling over her and brandishing his flogger. He let the soft leather straps dangle over her abdomen and the undersides of her breasts, teasing her skin with feathery promises that veiled painful intent. He fluttered them down her belly and inner thighs, then back up and over her breasts and shoulders. Eron winced slightly as the straps pulled a bit at the chain held in her mouth. The anticipation of being whipped was only heightened by the pressure of the clamps on her nipples, but even that pain was slowly budding into pleasure—like the hard, pinching fingers of a large, rough-hewn man's hands that refused to release the berry-pink centers of her breasts.

The flogger suddenly snapped out and lashed her belly. Eron grunted, rolling her eyes into her head from the combined agony and ecstasy of it. He beat her again, slapping her breasts with the long straps. Eron felt sure that the action would free one of her nipples with the sudden violence but again they held firm, tugging with an excruciatingly divine grip. The flogging suddenly became a whirlwind of flying straps peppering her skin. It beat down with furious speed and agility on her ribs, abdomen, inner thighs and quim. When Jatuu centered his attention on stimulating that moistening center with his marksmanship, Eron found herself panting and groaning, holding onto the chain in her teeth for dear life as her hips rolled and undulated.

Suddenly the flogger was a soft glove gliding over the surface of her skin again, giving Eron a chance to catch her breath. Her pussy was soaked in heat and wetness, and it hardly surprised her when her turned the whip over in his hands and began caressing her with its hardened end. Her toes curled and she cried out in pleasure when Eron's master first ran the whip's head down the cleft and hardened nub of her womanhood, then pressed the thick shaft up and into her. Despite her heightened arousal, the wide girth and leather texture of the flogger's handle made it a tight squeeze, and Jatuu savored every moment of pushing each inch deeper within her.

"AAH!" Eron squirmed and tried not to toss her head from side to side or twist her body for fear of tugging on the clamps holding her nipples imprisoned. When Jatuu slowly pulled the flogger back out of her, she could only clench her inner walls for a moment, forced to accept the object back into her again. He plunged it in with more speed and force this time, and soon he was jacking it in and out of her with vigor, one thick thumb of his powerful hand rubbing and twisting her hardened clitoris.

"Gods," she mumbled around the chain in her mouth. The world around her was forgotten—the whole of Shebwai could have been watching at that moment, and Eron wouldn't have cared, so expertly was this man pleasing her body. He pumped the phallus faster, quickly sending Eron over the edge. "Gods!" she screamed, but she never released the chain from her teeth, even when she threw her head back in rapture.

Jatuu pulled the phallic handle free of Eron, then took the chain from her mouth, tugging at her breasts himself. "Good," he granted, then settled himself between her still-spread legs and began rubbing his own hardened, dripping cock along Eron's clenched fists resting beneath the cleft of her buttocks. "Hmm," he said, seemingly getting an idea. "We shall have to turn you over and make sure every part of your body pleases me," he promised, "in a moment." He entered her effortlessly, pumping down into her while he took a moment to knead her captive breasts and grip Eron's throat and jaw. "You are truly beautiful, Eron," he told her while he fucked her. "You must still climax once more for me, though, or I shall have Laurallin beat you."

Pulling free of her before the tension between Eron's thighs could climb too high, Jatuu gripped his long, thick cock and ran it under the chain between Eron's breasts. He tugged at the chain once more, bringing her milky peaks together enough for him to begin sliding his slick manhood between them. When the glistening tip presented itself from between Eron's cleavage, she playfully licked it.

Jatuu released her long enough to flip her over bodily. Eron found herself facedown, her arms still bound against her sweaty backside now being thrust into the air. "Truly, you are exquisite." He continued to praise her form, entering her hot channel yet again once situated with his hands on her hips. "Your skin is flawless, your body is round and yet perfect. Such curves; soft, weighty breasts, supple legs, a smooth quim... Was your mother this beautiful?"

He could have been reciting the alphabet for all Eron cared at that moment with the things he was doing to her. She grinned and bit the pillow beneath her face, then moaned and ground her teeth when the clamps on her nipples pulled and swung.

Jatuu pulled free of her again. He was simply going through a ritual—lovemaking was a daily thing for this man, Eron knew, and the process and patterns of it were practiced with ease. The Sultan was marking his territory, though it did little to diminish the pleasure for either of them this night.

She could feel the swollen head of his throbbing prick move against her most secret spot with alarming pressure. Jatuu leaned over Eron's back, brushing her dark hair away with his mouth to breathe hotly into her ear. "Tonight I make you mine, Eron," he announced in a hiss against her lobe. He pushed, entering her anus with deliberate leisure, partly to savor it, and partly so as not to damage his new pet. Eron squeezed her eyes shut and groaned, a sound that even she could not distinguish as a pitiful '*no*,' or a wanton '*yes*.' She could feel him inside of her, filling her so completely in a way that drove her over the very edge.

"Yes!" he said triumphantly, pumping faster and spanking her ass. He gripped her long hair like reins and pulled, driving himself into her fully. Eron felt imprisoned in a new way—taken so bestially and bound against escape, yet wanting to be nowhere else in the entire world. She leaned towards him, meeting his thrusts and impaling herself onto him further.

"Yes!" Eron screamed.

"Yes, what?" he commanded, spanking her harder.

"Yes—Yes, Master!" She could feel her pussy convulse against the cock riding above it. "Oh, *Gods*—Yes, Master! Yes!" Jatuu reached around her thigh and found her clit with his fingers, and the single touch was all she needed. Eron exploded in a wash of heat and wetness, feeling her own juices drip down the thighs that threatened to give under her own weight. "Yes," she breathed against the cushions, then gasped aloud once more when Jatuu pulled his spurting rod out of her. She tipped sideways, lying in a crumpled, spent heap upon the sweaty pillows as she tried to catch her breath again.

"You pass," the Sultan told her. "I'll punish you no more—tonight."

"Yes, master," was all she managed to pant, but smiled at him.

Free of her bonds, Eron had been in Jatuu's arms for nearly a half hour, sitting nude in his embrace, eating grapes and watching the stars turn above them. She smiled at the slave standing beside them silently and took the offered glass. This sort of treatment, while nice after the sexual activities she had just endured, was certainly not what she expected. The stories and her own preconceptions and dreams of Shebwai, while perhaps right in some ways, did not even come close to preparing her for the true depth of Shebwai, and Eron knew she'd but scratched that surface.

The palace and its master were beautiful in their way, and deadly in others. Regardless, Eron relaxed in her lover's embrace, feeling both homesick and yet strangely content. The expanse of stars over the ocean brought thoughts of James and the look in his eyes the night before she had been sold. Eron sighed, deciding such longings would only get in the way.

"Master?" she asked, turning around in his arms.

"Yes?"

"May I sleep here with you this night?" She stroked his chest, but did not meet his eyes as she mewed her request. "I fear what Laurallin may do," she added, hoping to seal the deal.

"Very well," he nodded. "This night."

Eron smiled, nuzzling her head under his chin. She mentally patted herself on the back for her speedy accomplishments, finding herself on the lap of the Sultan of Shebwai, just as she had promised her King such a short time ago. Already she was working her way into his good graces and vying for his attentions against those that would leave her in a quiet corner where she could do nor hear anything that might help King Henrick's cause. Of course, being so close to Jatuu had its personal advantages; never in her life had she been treated to such opulence. It was a shame that she was a slave here. It might have been a nice challenge to instead have come here as an envoy or a betrothal, had circumstances been very different. Shebwai and its master had their own inner beauty that sang to a part of Eron she had never known existed. Such a rich culture deserved to be free, and she wouldn't have minded living amongst such freedom. And Jatuu himself was a magnificent lover—the evening had almost allowed Eron to finally put James out of her mind for the first time in days.

Things in Shebwai might not be so bad after all.

It was barely dawn when Eron awoke with a start. Given how late the Sultan had dragged her from the party it was entirely too early to be roused, as drunk and exhausted as she had been.

In the dim light she could instantly make out a male slave as he entered the room and dropped to his knees. The attending servants also started at the sudden intrusion, the whole scene waking Eron and the Sultan from where they lay on the giant bed. She sat up, still nude and collared, and pushed the hair from her swollen eyes to see what was transpiring.

"Forgive me, Holiness," the slave stammered. "He would not await for me to wake you."

"Who?" Eron wondered aloud, momentarily forgetting her place.

"Krel," Jatuu said angrily to himself. He rose, pulling on a pair of silk pants to hide his nudity just as a new figure stormed into the room. "What is it this time, Hanim?" he growled, his rage barely in check. "It had better be good."

Eron recognized the man who had stood at the Sultan's side the night before; the dark, cloaked figure that she had taken to be the infamous necromancer that had helped Jatuu rise to world power. The tall, broad-shouldered Hanim Krel nearly ran over the slave that had hastily announced him. He crossed his arms to regard the Sultan with disdain, regarding him almost as a disappointed father might look down on a loafing son. His eyes briefly met Eron's, then shot down to consume her nude state in a way that caused even her immodesty to shrivel away and wish to hide. Krel was staring at her even as he said in a thunderous, deep voice, "Your security is breached, Jatuu Olumbai. I warned you of this, bringing new faces into this house almost every day."

A cold fear gripped Eron's heart. Could this man already know of her agenda within the palace? She remained frozen in place, not wanted to call attention in the least.

"What are you talking about, wizard?" Jatuu asked. His eyes darted to Eron with uncertainty, obviously wondering why his trusted advisor was staring at a mere slave. "Speak with reason."

"I have discovered a spy within your home, Sultan," the necromancer hissed, finally tearing his gaze from Eron's breasts. "Where there is one so lowly there are sure to be others in higher places. Come and see what your lax behaviors have bought us," he said with a sweeping gesture toward the hall outside. Again the black figure with his equally night-shrouded cloak glanced at the Sultan's conquest, though if he somehow suspected Eron he made no motion to implicate her in whatever matter he referred to. She hoped that lust was the lesser of the evils that had caused Krel to stare at her so intently.

The Sultan left the bed's side at last, taking a moment to toss a thin, silken robe at Eron. She could do nothing but wrap the soft material around her slender shoulders and watch as her new master followed the wizard from the room. As soon as they had rounded the corner from the bedchamber, Eron moved to the corner of the bed closest to the exiting aperture, pulling at the collar keeping her chained in the room. She didn't care if the other slaves noticed her trying to catch either sight or sound of what transpired outside; their own curiosity was surely piqued, and Eron shared a bed with the man. She was surely justified in openly eavesdropping from her bound position.

A light suddenly illuminated the hallway where the Sultan and his necromancer stood, gazing down on whatever it was that Krel was showing Jatuu. Eron could only guess that the light was from a wizard's spell. It threw the two imposing figures into silhouette, and suddenly Eron was able to make out another figure lying in a crumpled heap just beyond the doorway.

Eron could see that there he was a young man in the garb of a servant and apparently unconscious. "A spy," Hanim Krel said with a dramatic wave of his hand at his captive. "He is a Kingdom agent," he said, adding, "*Holiness.*"

For the briefest instant Eron thought she might faint.

"There can be only more of these roaches within your home," Krel continued angrily. "This jeopardizes everything! Now I must spend valuable time torturing this one in order to track the others."

"Keep your voice down!" Jatuu commanded. The conversation was continued in harsh whispers, and although Eron strained to hear what transpired she could make out nothing of value. She wrapped her thin covering around her body, shivering despite the warm night.

At last Krel turned away, dragging his unconscious prisoner behind him and muttering to himself in a dialect Eron had never before heard. She backed towards the head of her cushioned prison and settled as though she had never moved. Moments later Jatuu returned silently, climbing in to bed next to her.

With a sudden forcefulness than nearly caused Eron to scream he tore the silk robe from her body and smothered her in a forceful grasp. "Breath not a word of this night to anyone," Jatuu commanded. His words were simple, but the look in his eyes held a promise of death or worse should he be disobeyed. Of that, Eron was certain. A shudder all but wracked her body, so sure and cold was Jatuu's eyes and demeanor. She nodded and swallowed, wondering what he might do next.

Eron worried briefly that he might take out the frustrations of the last few minutes on her flesh. Instead he turned her around bodily and wrapped an arm over her, pressing his warm body against her naked back and settling in for sleep. Eron's eyes darted about, but no terrible fate materialized to envelope her. Her stiff spine relaxed when Jatuu's hand suddenly caressed her hair, instructing her to go back to sleep. The ministration was brief but welcome.

And just like that Eron's emotions were again challenged by complications. One form or another, her enemies were in this palace, and Eron knew she must not forget that, no matter how it pained her or how lovely her surroundings and their master might make her feel.

Fingers massaged Eron's shoulders and neck, then cupped the round globes of her breasts. Everything about James's lovemaking was superbly soft except for his rigid cock, pinning her back against the rough pumice stone. Even the vine-like strands of seaweed that held Eron bound naked to the rocks had a wet, welcome feel. Anchored impossibly close to the tiny island of jutting pumice was the *Angry Goddess*, rolling silently in the warm sea. The crashing waves sprayed the pirate captain's naked body, and the water rolled off of his bronzed skin and dark hair to drip onto Eron's breasts and belly. She writhed in abandon beneath his touch as the spray caused her hair to stick to her skin. As James's shaft began grounding Eron down against the painful surface of the island she grinned, realizing that she was indeed stuck between 'a rock and a hard place.' It was torturously wondrous.

James spent himself within her, his tongue invading her mouth as they both moaned in climax. Smiling, he looked deep into her eyes for just a moment before rising off of her to stand proud and naked. Eron pulled at the vines to join him, but found the growth to be not only restraining her fast against the isle, but also now pulling languorously at her limbs to secure her even tighter. No words could escape her still-tingling lips; only breathy sounds of excitement and fear uttered from her.

James grinned happily and turned, springing still nude into the shimmering waters of the impossibly vast ocean. Eron watched helplessly as he swam to the ship and then climbed its side. No one came to its side to watch her struggle as the *Goddess* turned into the sunset and set sail for the horizon.

The seaweed wrapped tighter about Eron's wrists and ankles even as it spread her limbs wider, scraping them along the pumice. Panic gripped the Lady of Tibeth's heart as she realized she was being left behind. The spray of the waves became a drenching assault on her body. The water teased mercilessly at her still-swollen nipples and exposed clit, now left so open by the forcing apart of Eron's legs. Even as the true gravity of her helplessness began to overcome Eron the scenario worsened—the waterline was rising quickly, sinking her tiny island into the sea with her bound steadfastly to it. Still she had no breath to scream, for the constant barrage of the ocean's dripping water blinded her and all but drowned her even as the level rose up the incline to consume first Eron's feet, then lap her naked calves and thighs. Soon only her face and jutting breasts broke the quivering grip of the water. Eron trembled and squeezed her eyes tight, realizing that in a moment she would be completely beneath the water's warm grasp...

Eron's gasping caused the servants still waiting in the Sultan's bedroom to start once more. Realizing her surroundings and that the day had come, Eron moved to rise from the bed, finding instead that the leash still bound her to the bed. Before a moan of exasperation could utter from Eron's frustrated visage a harem girl appeared with a key.

"I am Sacha," she said with a perfect Kingdom accent as she released Eron from the leash. "I am to show you our quarters."

"Ours?" Eron asked with genuine interest. She remembered Sacha's name from her conversation with Embeth and the other slaves. This pretty, lithe youth with her blonde hair and unblemished skin was said to be the Sultan's favorite next to that bitch Laurallin.

"Yes. You are favored in our Master's eyes." She grinned and took Eron's hand, helping her from the giant bed. "Which means un-favored in the Harem Overseer's view. Unless you wish to see her today, I suggest you hasten with me. Laurallin often returns to shower the Master's bed with rose petals or whatever nonsense reminds him of her existence."

Eron laughed at that, finding the expression fresh and needed after the hardships of the past few days. "You are from the Kingdoms?" she asked as she dressed in a thin wrap that Sacha provided. She secured it between her breasts and paused in a mirror to study her collar and tangled hair.

"My mother was from Granelayde. I was captured by a convoy of desert tradesmen years ago," Sacha answered with a simple smile. If the memory brought pain, she showed not even the slightest hint of it. "My father, a lord of the Southern Province, had taken us on an expedition to hunt lions. The nomads killed my father and his litter-bearers. I became a slave of the chief at 15, and a few years later he sold me to the Shebwai market for a small fortune," she laughed slightly, "which the chief needed by then. He wasn't a very good tradesman."

"I see," was all Eron could think to say. Any thoughts that this young woman might be an agent or connection for her quickly dissipated.

"But there are others here like us," Sacha continued lightly, and Eron nodded with renewed interest. "I will introduce you later. First, let us get you cleaned up and ready for the day."

Glancing back at the empty bed in the center of the sunlit chamber, Eron tried to ignore the lingering thoughts and fear that had been assailing her ever since that wizard Krel had invaded her mind with his very presence. With concerns and dreams still conflicting her, Eron left the bedroom and followed her new roommate away.

Chapter 11

Eron wondered if the wicker fan blades above her head turned by means of slave labor or a magic spell. She was always bored at the prospect of simply lying about, and frustrated by waiting for others to decide her fate. Eron sighed and played absently with the jewels hanging from her skimpy garments, rolling over on her palette to stare for the third time that hour at the room's colorful floor.

"You look troubled." Sacha said from the palette beside her own. "Shall we go play with the others?" she asked without lowering her book.

Eron couldn't read the strange scribbles of the Shebwai language, but she didn't wish to be among a group of tittering girls either. Two weeks in the Harem of the Sultan of Shebwai had passed, though it was not always like this. Eron's loneliness and worry of discovery had been supplemented by her time with Jatuu; at least six of the fourteen nights of her captivity she had slept in his arms. The sex had ranged from the Sultan's dominant commanding of his submissive to passionate and arousing love play that had left Eron fighting to hold her emotions in check.

Still, Eron's worries deepened. While people like Sacha and Embeth were kind in their way, and Jatuu was intriguingly powerful and mysterious, no agents from the Kingdom had contacted Eron. She told herself that living in the wing of the Harem closest to the Sultan's own apartments made her hard to get to, so she wandered the halls as often as she could hoping to stumble across her hidden allies. She dreaded that Krel may have discovered them, fearing that she might never get back out of the palace and Shebwai.

And then there was the matter of finding Corine.

Memories of James had faded into a dull ache and a recurring dream of being lost at sea or drowned on the rock isle as the *Goddess* sailed out of reach. She tried not to dwell on her feelings for the pirate captain, as it only made it harder to be alone in the harem or to concentrate when she was with the Sultan. Fortunately she had managed to avoid Laurallin most of the time. Eron's existence, while one of captivity and bondage, was rarely unpleasant, truly, though she doubted that would last. A woman like Laurallin would find a way to vengeance. She also knew that she would have to learn more of her captors soon, and that meant being even closer to Jatuu, and worse—learning the secrets of the necromancer Krel and his allegiance with the Sultan.

"You are worried about Corine again?" Sacha asked.

"No," Eron said, rolling to her back and staring this time at the beautifully tiled ceiling of their room. "Yes. I don't know. There has been much to adjust to. Perhaps I simply have been in the rooms of the harem too long. The only time I get to see the sky I am in the bedroom and I am supposed to be looking into our Master's eyes or staring at the floor in submission."

"Ah," Sacha said, holding up a finger. "I may be able to help you there." She rose and took Eron's hand. "Come."

Eron watched Sacha's slender hips and perfect ass swagger as she walked on her bare toes as though she were wearing heels. "Sacha," she asked, "why has his holiness not yet made Laurallin or yourself Sultana?"

"Why—do you think you can do better than she or I at winning his love?" Sacha's voice had been quiet, but there was now an icy air to it.

"No! No," Eron apologized quickly, "I ask as to the Sultan's demeanor towards the women of the Harem, not to insult you."

Sacha's lips twisted into a knowing smile, but her voice returned to its original liquored warmth. "His Holiness is too preoccupied with plans for the world to waste time thinking about taking a bride. He and that black demon Hanim Krel spend much of their time together, making plans over maps or yelling at generals. We are but a distraction to end our master's hard day."

The halls of the palace became quiet and shadowed as they moved out of the main corridors and away from where most of the staff congregated. Sacha smiled over her shoulder once and held up a finger for silence as she led her roommate to a dark alcove at the end of a forgotten hallway. At the back of the alcove was another narrow passage, this one leading out into a shaft of light. Eron found herself blinking away tears, squinting up at the sun that was baking the small, walled area.

"The Harem may be a lavish place of baths and pools surrounded by jeweled lattices and golden tiles, but it is a prison nonetheless. This," Sacha said with a knowing incline of her nose, "is the only place where we can even get *close* to the outside world now."

She was standing in a tiny courtyard made of two palace walls joining at a right angle, a few plants, and a high, barred fence that looked out onto a city alleyway between two portions of the palace's outer walls. The fence was several stories tall and spiked at the top, and another fence was five feet away, making certain that Eron could not even touch the outside world. The walls above were sheer and unable to be climbed.

In the alleyway, there was a woman waiting in long robes and a veil. She lowered the veil and stood the moment Eron fallowed Sacha to the edge of the courtyard.

It was Corine.

Eron nearly gasped aloud. She quickly turned to Sacha, grinning at the harem girl excitedly. "This is wonderful. Thank you!" She hugged the girl and almost forcibly turned her away. "Do you mind if I stay here a moment—alone?"

"Do not linger too long," Sacha warned. "We're not really supposed to come out here," she added, eyeing the cloaked figure beyond with suspicion. Sacha finally turned and left.

Eron ran to the bars, reaching for her friend's hands but finding the distance to great to touch her. "How did you find me?"

"I've been coming here for days in the hopes that you would find me, mistress," Corine said quietly, though her smile was beaming. "One of the other serving girls in the Marjah's household has a sister in the Sultan's Harem, and told me this is how she visits her."

Eron felt happier than she had in days to see her friend. "Are you treated well? I see they let you out of the house," she added with a laugh.

"I'm told the Marjah that bought me is an uncommon man." Corrine's smile faded a little. "He can be indifferent to the household duties and those who perform it sometimes. A mistress tells me what to do or where I can go most of the time." She blushed a little as she added, "But then the master really bought me as an evening's diversion. Since then, I've just been busy trying to find you."

Smiling appreciatively, Eron leaned her head on the bars that separated her from her friend. "I'm thankful for that. But I don't have much time. I've not…" She stopped, checking herself before she could say anything that might be overheard. She continued in a whisper. "I've not met any friends from the kingdoms, and I don't know when the Sultan may tire of me. I miss freedom." She looked Corine in the eyes, making sure she was conveying her message as clearly as possible. "What of my captain?"

Corine leaned as close as she could, glancing around behind Eron's back as she whispered. "I still see the masts of the *Goddess* in the harbor, Eron. He must still be awaiting repairs."

"Then at least there is that hope," Eron replied, breathing a sigh.

"Eron," Corine said, her brow furrowing. "What are you going to do?"

"I don't know," Eron admitted. "But I should start passing you notes, at the very least. Perhaps the captain can do me a favor, as he brought me here." She smiled, trying to alleviate her friend's fears. "Meet me here tomorrow, same time. We'll talk more." She reached out. "Farewell till then, Corine."

"Farewell, mistress."

Eron turned, hurrying back towards the dark aperture that opened out onto this tiny slice of heaven.

It was Hell the moment she stepped inside.

Laurallin grabbed Eron by the shoulders and pressed her against the wall. "Who was that girl?" she demanded. She had been waiting in the hall just beyond the courtyard, but Eron didn't know for how long or what she might have overheard. "What in hell do you think you're doing coming here?" Her grip became even harder, nearly bruising Eron's flesh.

"Let go of me," Eron spat, trying to twist free. "No one said that this place was forbidden."

"Who was that girl?" Laurallin repeated, angrier this time.

"A serving wench from some Marjah's home," Eron said without lying. "Now unhand me before you leave a mark that the Sultan would find."

"You think I could not beat you whenever I please," the harem-mistress said with an evil grin. "You're mine when you're not in his bedchamber. You've been talking with an outsider, and I'd just as soon punish you myself as tell the Sultan of your transgression."

"Then do so," Eron challenged, "or release me now, or so help me I'll scratch that grin off your face."

"You're more than you seem, bitch," Laurallin hissed, "And I'll find the truth of you." Then, surprisingly, she released Eron's arms.

Eron stared back only a moment before taking her chance to storm off and avoid an immediate beating. Laurallin might not have dared to punish Jatuu's new favorite just yet, but that woman was forming plans, and Eron would have to be careful. A rather impossible prospect, given the fact that her meeting with Corine made her realize that she needed to work on her mission fast, regardless of whether or not she was trapped in the palace forever.

Eron searched desperately for someplace that a harem girl was allowed to be alone, if even for just a moment. She would let no one see the tears welling in her eyes if she could help it, and to let those tears fall unbidden would be a shame greater than any public beating Laurallin or the Sultan himself could muster up. Eron found a corner somewhere between the doors leading into the Harem Wing and the Bathhouse, avoiding the guards on the other side. She turned away so as not to let anyone see her lose control so desperately. Eron pressed her shivering, barely clad body into the dark corner and released her feelings at last.

She wept as silently as she could, stifling the sobs and sniffling as little as possible. Eron hated feeling trapped anywhere, but she had managed to fool herself until now. Such denial was no longer available to her, though, and Eron was certain she was alone and lost in the palace until Henrick of Capriana himself brought the armies of the Kingdoms to the Sultan's doors.

Seeing Corine and being confronted by that woman who dared to command and threaten her had been all it took to drag the last vestiges of her resolve to the depths—she had to cry it all out now or she would never be able to risk her life further and get valuable information to Corine and hopefully the King. She let it all out through giant tears and gulps for breath over the course of many long minutes, until finally Eron was able to regain her composure enough to turn away from the wall and wipe the moisture from her swollen eyes.

"You are scared."

Eron jumped, bringing her hands to her mouth to check an involuntary cry. Standing before her was Hanim Krel, the Sultan's necromancer. She had not heard the doors to the Harem wing open or a single footstep on the flagstones, yet there he stood. As always, he was the most imposing figure she had ever seen, standing like a giant black wall that barred her from fleeing in any direction.

"H-how did you…" Eron started. She mustered her poise once more, remembering just whom she was while trying her best not to bring the thoughts of her home to mind lest this monstrous man could read them like an open book. "You're not allowed in the Harem."

"I tread wherever I like on this world," Krel said in his deep voice. He smiled, "Even in this palace." He advanced on her, a look on his dark features somewhere between bestial stalking and intense study. "What scares you, kingdom whore? The Sultan? His mistresses? His dominance? His world?" He reached for her shoulder, and Eron pulled away, certain that one touch could somehow lock her into his servitude forever. "Could it be me?"

Eron backed against the wall, her palms searching the cold tiles behind her for a way out while her eyes never left the hulking form of her tormentor. "I am a slave, but I am the Sultan's slave, not yours. I don't have to tell you anything of my fears."

Krel stood over her, so close that she could feel his breath on her cheek, but he did not reach for her. "You should. You should tell me everything." His eyes caressed her, and he placed his hands on the wall either side of her, cutting of her escape and turning Eron's legs to jelly. His beard was almost brushing her skin. "You are very beautiful. What is your name?"

"Eron." The breathy response came unbidden to her lips.

"Eron," he repeated sweetly. "Eron, which kingdom were you from?"

"Capriana," she answered, hoping that a truth would put him off his suspicions.

"Ah, the first Kingdom." He shook his head sadly, and pulled away from her at last. Eron's held breath came out as a heaving sigh as soon as he averted his gaze for a moment. Krel's voice became hard again. "Then I will never truly win your heart—you are entirely too close to this matter and will hate me after the week is out."

Both revelations, though cryptic, turned Eron's blood to ice. Did he suspect her? Did he mean to have her? And what did he plan against Capriana that seemed so certain to him that would cause her to hate the necromancer further? "What do you mean?" she dared to ask him.

But Krel only smiled. "Come. You can lead me to your master—that way he will believe I was brought in properly." Again his eyes became as death and he stared into Eron's very soul. "If you speak of this matter to His Holiness, I will take great pleasure in killing you, Eron." He leaned back, smiling again. With a gesture of his hand, he bade her lead the way.

Eron kept her back straight and her gaze down as she entered her master's bedroom and knelt before Jatuu. "Hanim Krel begs audience, master."

The sultan raised an eyebrow but said evenly, "Very well." He set down his quill.

Krel breezed in and came to stand menacingly behind the bowed form of Eron. "I leave tonight, Holiness. I shall return in two days."

Eron could sense Jatuu's smile as he answered, "Our plans move forward. Very well. Go forth with my blessings and do not fail."

With a sweep of his cloak that brushed Eron's backside as though on purpose, Krel bowed and left the room. "Shall I leave, master?" Eron asked when he was gone.

"No," Jatuu said. You may dine with Laurallin and me."

Eron's eyes became as wide as saucers, but she bit her lip before voicing her distaste, and fear, at the notion.

James had thought it would get easier with each passing day, but it had only become harder. Eron was near, in the same city as he and at the mercy of other men's wants and desires, but nowhere in sight and with no hope of return. Her scent still lingered on his sheets, her face haunted his dreams, and the feel of her hair between his fingers was a sensation that his mind would not release. James could only shake his head at such useless frustrations and light his pipe, staring longingly at the repairs to the hole in his cabin that had jarred his realization.

He loved her—and he hated her for it.

Once before in his life had James thought he had been in love. It was, as with so many men, the time spent with his first lover that had brought forth such ideals. Similarities between the youthful couple had had little bearing on his feelings for Sheila—she had been young, passionate, and fun to be around. But she was older than he at sixteen by three full years. When James had confessed what he thought were his true feelings, Sheila had told him in no uncertain terms whom she had her heart set on; the port's most-revered first mate would return soon. The man would be promoted to captain within a year, and then she would be his to marry. Realizing that he had been a diversion, James had left in pain and disgust, vowing to never again feel so deeply for another. Love had never been a need before or since that day—until now.

James took a long drag off of the wooden pipe, letting the sweetly flavored smoke fill his mouth and swirl about his beard and hair before he exhaled the remains. Love was not an emotion he was going to admit to outwardly, but the truth was inescapable. He missed Eron, he wanted her back, and he wanted out of the damnable port and the bargain with the devil that had stuck him there in the first place. A devil that for all James knew had his bonny love in his lap at that very moment.

"*I'm going to free us,*" Eron had told him.

James wondered just what she had meant.

"It's coming along." It was Telorn, standing behind him and gesturing at the repairs to the main cabin. When James didn't answer, the first mate said, "I saw the girl, Corine, yesterday."

"You did *what?*" James demanded, wheeling on his friend with naked anger. "Are you trying to get us all killed?"

Telorn's face was sternly unapologetic, but he held up his hands in supplication. "I saw her by chance, from across a market in the daylight business hours. I didn't get a chance to talk to her before she was gone, but I won't say I didn't want to."

James relaxed a little at that. In truth, he now wished Telorn had been able to talk to Eron's friend and find out how she was doing. It was comforting to know, at least, that he was not the only one longing for the women they had been forced to sell. "How did she look?" he finally managed to ask without sounding contemptuous.

"Like the slave of a rich Shebwai bastard—properly healthy, bejeweled and veiled despite being clad in next to nothing under her cloak."

"At least she's healthy," James grumbled.

"Aye," Telorn replied dryly.

"Do you think you could find her again?" James asked.

Telorn studied his captain a moment before responding. "No—unfortunately. At least, not easily." The mate turned his eyes heavenward and made a show of studying the progressing repairs. "Has the foreman said how much longer we'll be here?"

"In no certain terms," James answered. "Not long, though. The city is gearing for war—another invasion and another province or kingdom shall fall to the might of Shebwai. We should leave soon and avoid the tempered anger that comes with war." He looked Telorn in the eye. "*If* you're going to try and find her, make it quick, and don't take her until we're ready to sail on the tide."

Telorn simply nodded in agreement. "Aye, Cap'n." He turned away without another word, leaving James to his own thoughts of women and the darkness each turn of the world brought; Darkened night, like Eron's hair in the moonlight.

"Eron," James breathed.

Eron," Laurallin commanded from where she sat nestled against the Sultan, "kneel."

Eron did as she was bade, kneeling with her head bowed and her hands clasped behind her back. Clad now only in a tiny thong and her jewels, she could feel the warmth of Sacha's body next to hers. The lithe blonde harem girl was dressed only slightly less revealing than Eron, her small breasts confined by a tiny strip of cloth and her legs encased by billowing, transparent pantaloons. She had been brought in via leash only moments before the feast for the Sultan had been wheeled in on giant platters. Now both slaves awaited the pleasures of their master and his favorite, and Laurallin was smiling in a way that suggested a long evening of humiliation.

"By your leave, Master," Laurallin begged of Jatuu, bowing as she glanced menacingly at the two slaves.

"Yes," the Sultan said off handedly. "Do as you will."

Jatuu smiled, though his thoughts seemed to be on anything but the girls awaiting him. He stared with a faraway look that made Eron feel alone and alienated. The Sultan was dreaming of power and possibilities, Eron knew, and it was a power that made his desires very different from hers, and very dangerous. Once more, Eron longed for James, wishing she had never left his arms to come to this alien place and the struggle and confusion it held. Perhaps it would have been better to live even a few final months at sea with James and a feeling of freedom and happiness than to be left feeling so stuck and hopeless.

Laurallin was removing her own skimpy top and blatantly pinching her own nipples into erection as she looked down on the harem girls on the floor. She popped a grape into their master's mouth before dining on her own. She then nestled her head onto Jatuu's shoulder like a kitten, taking care to brush only the bare skin of his chest with her long hair and not let it stray into his food. "Sacha," she commanded, "Stand. Pick up the crop."

Sacha did as bade and came to stand behind Eron, whose breathing quickened.

"Eron, kneel erect and keep your hands at the small of your back." Laurallin reached out to continue feeding her master, moaning a little as she continued to flick and roll her right nipple between her fingers and mew against Jatuu's side. Eron could only obey, rising from where her ass rested on her calves, leaving it open to beating. She prepared herself for what was coming.

"Now strike, Sacha," Laurallin commanded. Sacha's riding crop with its palm-like end slapped against the bare right cheek of Eron's backside. She bit her lip and grunted against the pain of it, reminded of how good and how painful the device could feel. "Again. Again!"

The Sultan hardly seemed to notice either Laurallin's ministrations or the spectacle she commanded, concentrating on eating what he was fed while staring out across the chamber and into space.

What could he be thinking, Eron wondered of her current lover. Word had spread through the harem of mobilization of troops and the whispers within the city of an escalation to the war. Hanim Krel's words and threatening posture, to say nothing of his sexual advances, had only made Eron's fears for her homeland worse. She was surrounded by plotters, unable to find allies, and lost to a Sultan who may be dreaming up new plans of destruction while he gazed upon her supplicant flesh and commanded her through a sadistic, slave-driving bitch. For all Eron knew, Laurallin might hand Eron over to the Necromancer personally if ever given the chance. Just as chilling was the thought that the evil bastard might have killed her only contact within the palace and would torture and kill her if he ever knew the truth.

And there sat Jatuu, a man she might have grown to truly respect and care for if he weren't so hell-bent of conquering the world—or if Eron ever truly gave in to submission. The same homeland so far away that was the cause of her fears was the only true anchor she could cling to now to keep her panic down. Remembering the teachings of the *Chateau*, Eron willed her posture and mind to accept her decisions, find power through her submission, and the strength once more to get through all of this. If only she were alone with the Sultan and not trapped with his debouched slaves; with the Necromancer mysteriously gone she might have dared to pick Jatuu for clues to his plans.

Eron knew her cheeks must be red and hot by now after the repeated spankings from the crop. A tiny gasp or a squeal of delightful pain was forced from her lungs with each strike, but her mind stayed centered on her mission and escape. She glanced up through her long lashes at her master and mistress, hating Laurallin for the smirk on her lips. It might have been worth it if Jatuu was at least paying attention, but he was eating heartily of his meal and thinking of whatever terrors either his army or his necromancer would unleash upon the world soon. With each hollow sting of the crop Eron hated the Sultan for his thoughts but still wanted him to watch and perhaps gain pleasure.

Anything would have been better than giving Laurallin satisfaction with this show, Eron thought, trying to rationalize the moment. But the truth was that she wanted Jatuu to watch, to want her, to be pleased by her and pleasured along with her. Instead she could do nothing as Laurallin added insult to injury by reaching down to free the Sultan's erect penis and begin stroking him slowly. Meanwhile her free hand left her own breasts and slipped beneath the ties of her shorts and quest between her rubbing, hot thighs. With shame and trepidation, Eron realized that Laurallin was going to make the most of this.

"Stop," Laurallin commanded breathlessly. When Sacha seemed not to hear over the exquisite sounds of her quickened strikes, the harem mistress repeated, "Sacha, stop. Remove your pants and retrieve a strapped phallus."

Eron's eyes widened, though she dared not look up at the Sultan with the horror or pleading that she wished she could communicate. To do so would invite a worse fate, she knew. Laurallin would use any excuse she could while at Jatuu's side to have Eron chained and beaten worse. She would have to turn this to her advantage and get back at Laurallin another way.

Eron knew what was coming next even before the Harem Mistress's words came. Laurallin had pushed the small tables and platters aside so that she might kneel before Jatuu and perform fellatio. She then grasped the Sultan's cock and after one enticing lick along the shaft looked over her shoulder at Eron with an evil grin. She pushed her thin pants down off of her hips and all but wagged her naked rear at the helpless slave. "Pleasure me, Kingdom whore," she commanded. "Crawl up these steps and pleasure me as Sacha takes you."

Eron chanced a look over at Sacha, who looked noncommittal to the affair as she finished tying a large porcelain phallus onto her waist as though it were her own. The girl waited for Eron to obey the order before positioning herself behind her.

Laurallin was already feasting on Jatuu's cock, forcing his wayward attention down on her. "Look at me, master," she begged while looking up at him with dark, almost commanding eyes. She licked the underside of his balls then slurped hungrily on his rod, forcing him to close his eyes in pleasure at last. "I am yours, master."

Eron had crawled up the steps as ordered, determined to make the most of the humiliating moment. Hate for Laurallin was put aside when she finished pulling the mistress's pants down to her knees and regarded the shapely, dusky hued backside of the older but attractive woman. She could smell Laurallin's need and feel her own juices flowing from the sting of the crop. Eron gasped again when Sacha's soft hands rested on her red, still-smarting ass, announcing that the strap-on was about to take her from behind for the Sultan's viewing pleasure. Eron waited until the thick length of the dildo had entered her before delving her face between Laurallin's cheeks, groaning in lusty abandon as the device filled her and began fucking her.

Laurallin glanced back to watch as the kingdom slave moved down to lick at her from where she knelt. The Harem Mistress laughed, then returned to her own oral fixations.

Eron lapped at Laurallin's pussy and nestled her face between the hot globes of her ass. She rocked back and forth on her knees as she was taken by another woman. Eron let the eroticism and carnal desires of the moment drown out the shame of why and how it was happening.

Sacha grasped Eron's hands still clasped behind her, riding her harder while striking her naked back with the crop and pulling at her long brown tresses. The lithe blonde was getting into it now as well, throwing her head back and forth and thrusting away like a horny angel.

"You serve me well," Jatuu said to no one in particular. The Sultan was watching through heavily lid eyes at last, gazing down at the women pleasuring each other and, finally, serving his cock. It was all Eron needed to gather the desire and courage to do what she herself wanted.

Laurallin's quim was drenched in her own juices and the wetness of Eron's hot mouth. Eron gently removed her hands from behind her back to help support her weight and insert two fingers into the mistress's pussy. "Oh!" Laurallin exclaimed, grinding down on the intruding digits. Eron grinned and quested deeper with her tongue. The intoxicating musk of the orgy was whipping them all into a frenzied state, so she hoped no one would notice her take the initiative until it was too late.

Eron kept one hand dedicated to pleasuring Laurallin while she dared to meet Jatuu's gaze at last. She licked her way along the perfect curve of her mistress's ass to her lower back, leaving a sticky trail of hot saliva and juices all the way, stopping to smile up at her goal. She locked eyes with Jatuu in a way that she knew was wrong for a slave, which made it all the more intriguing for him— just as the first time he had taken her. Jatuu smiled back, oblivious now to the mistress left slurping in abandon between his thighs.

Never even blinking while she gazed up and smiled, Eron slid free of Sacha's strapped-on phallus and motioned back for her to join in on her coup. Still on her knees, Eron's juices glistening on the large phallus, Sacha obeyed, coming up behind the kingdom woman's back and silently waiting. Eron drew aside to allow the young blonde access to Laurallin, helping her guide the hot dildo into the mistress's most secret place.

"Ah!" Laurallin screamed, her eyes squeezed shut as she let the new invader fill her to the hilt. She knelt back, impaling herself while absently holding Jatuu's shaft.

Eron took the moment to rise and straddle their master's lap, wrapping her arms around Jatuu's neck. She smiled as Laurallin was left unintentionally holding his cock in place for Eron to slide down onto him. "Mmm," she groaned, filling herself, and she kissed Jatuu deeply.

"You play with fire," Jatuu whispered with a smile. The Sultan returned Eron's kiss with open desire, stopping only to relieve Laurallin's pause of shock by commanding, "Continue."

Eron, now given open permission, began riding the Sultan to climax. "Yes!"

Eron rode faster, feeling her own orgasm coming on. She rolled her hips and presented her own backside to Laurallin with a knowing smile. Still lost somewhere between rage and desire, the woman surrendered to the latter when Sacha quickened the pace of anally fucking the harem mistress and spanking her with the crop. Agape, Laurallin's open mouth finally lowered down to nestle between Eron's pink cheeks. With that, she began licking the only orifice still open to her. When Laurallin inserted a finger as well, Eron could take no more. "Yes, yes... Oh, GODS, yes!" she screamed, shuddering in Jatuu's embrace as she bucked and shook on his lap.

Jatuu grunted, lifting Eron's still trembling flesh from his loins just in time to climax. His seed squirted into the air from his twitching cock, sending hot streams onto Laurallin's reddened face. She gasped and let the hot cum glaze her skin, digging her nails into Jatuu's thighs as she climaxed as well. Fucked into submission, the harem mistress could only lean against her master's knees as he settled Eron back down onto his lap.

"I believe you've earned your right to a meal, my little law-breaker," he told Eron. He gestured to the platters. "You may have your fill. Laurallin, you have eaten. If Sacha is to have her portion, she must first have her fill." He gestured to where Sacha knelt in silence. "Bring her to orgasm."

Laurallin looked up through tangled strands of wet hair from tear-soaked eyes, but said only, "Yes, Master," in quiet agreement. She turned obediently to the arms of Sacha, never kissing the younger slave as she began to do her best to please her body.

Eron almost felt sorry for Laurallin at that moment.

Almost.

Chapter 12

Corine ran down the alley. She hoped to the gods that no one found her, or that no fiend might be hiding in the dark corners to abduct her. The sun was still in the hot, bleached sky, but that would not stop someone this far from the main streets from doing whatever they wanted with her. The Marjah she had been sold to may have had his niceties, but she doubted that they ranged as far as paying a ransom for Corine if cutthroats captured her. Fortunately she had been allowed freedom enough to seek out Eron once more at the courtyard behind the palace. Corine just hoped that she had enough time to take whatever information her mistress might provide her back to the harbor and the *Angry Goddess*.

All of this suffering away from home must come to some good, she prayed.

Such hopes were dashed against hot stone the moment Corine found that the alley now ended in a wall. A wall of rock and stucco had replaced the barred fence that had once looked onto the enclosed courtyard virtually overnight. Too tall and steep to climb, Corine knew it meant the end of communicating with Eron for as long as she was a prisoner of the Sultan. She stifled a sob of despair and paced the narrow alley for long moments, lost in desperate thought. Finally, she resigned herself to the only possibility left open to her. Corine ran headlong, back out of the alley and into the streets of Shebwai, heading for the harbor and the forest of ship's masts she could just make out from the top of the hill.

Eron stared in speechless horror. Between the two fences of the courtyard facing the alley, a wall had been erected, and it had been put there so that she could never again talk to the outside world.

Thoughts reeled through Eron's mind. Was her role as a Kingdom agent suspected? Had the Sultan himself ordered the wall built overnight? Should Eron have never dared to play so rough with Laurallin's emotions while still trying to spy and get information out of the palace?

It mattered little now; the die had been cast and Eron was alone with her mistakes. She could only hope that somehow Corine could get word back to James for someone to eventually get her out before she was killed. If there were still other agents within the palace, she would discover anything she could of the Sultan's plans and get it to them, or eventually die trying to escape.

"How unfortunate," came a quiet, insincere voice from behind Eron. It was not, as Eron had suspected, Laurallin standing there when she turned, but the blonde Kingdom slave.

"Sacha?" Eron cried out in disbelief. "You did this?"

Sacha shrugged and acted unconcerned. "I told Laurallin yesterday that you came out here," she admitted. "I figured she would do the rest."

"Why?" Eron tried dreadfully not to let the tears welling in her large eyes to course down her hot cheeks, but they came unbidden.

"Because," she answered simply. "I had only to wait for the Sultan to tire of Laurallin—but once you came, there were instantly murmurs that I now had to vie against you as well for the Sultan's favor. If ever he takes a Sultana it shall be me, and at last I shall be taken out into the world again, as a queen." Sacha turned away. "As much as I hate being alone, I want you out of my room, Eron. Tonight."

"You're a fool, Sacha," Eron told her. "You've given up the freedom for either of us against the vain chance he'll never tire of you."

"What do you know? You're just an arrogant diva." With that, she disappeared back into the narrow alcove that led back into the palace.

Eron was left alone with her fears and loss. The thought of Sacha reduced to conspiring with Laurallin quickly enraged Eron, and she spent the next few minutes channeling that just to gain the strength to re-enter the palace and face the world that she had enslaved herself to. When her anger subsided, she was again left hollow and determined, though even a woman as resourceful as Eron was now without so much as an idea as to what to do next. *At least,* she thought hopefully, *Laurallin hadn't ordered the entire courtyard closed off from the light of the sun.*

Corine noted with fear the long shadows she was casting and looked to where the sun was about to disappear behind the city of Shebwai. She quickened her pace, hoping that no soldier would stop her from getting to the harbor to question her. She would be missed at the Marjah's household, but Corine could come up with an excuse by then, she knew. She had to somehow find her way to the *Angry Goddess*; that was all that mattered now.

By the time the shadows had dimmed to the purple haze of twilight, she had stumbled onto the pier and made her way towards the familiar kingdom-style masts of the ship that had brought her to this accursed land. Corine was exasperated to find no docking plank to allow her access to the deck, so she risked calling out to anyone who might be aboard. "Hello!" she called up hastily. "Please, is anyone there?"

"There's no one there who will answer," came a rough, accented voice from a nearby doorway. A small, old Shebwai man stepped from the shadows of the harbor foreman's house and approached her. "The only ones aboard are sleeping or guarding the ship," he told her, letting out a final puff of smoke from his pipe before dumping its ashen contents upon the pier. "I am Azim. Who are you, if not a Kingdom woman?"

"I am cursed," she answered. "A stranger here who can find no friends if they are not on that ship."

Azim smiled comfortingly. "If you seek the captain or his mate, then I can at least point you in the right direction."

Corine beamed with renewed happiness. "Yes. Oh, yes, please."

"Down the pier you will find an inn with the sign of the *Speared Grahrk*."

Corine almost laughed at the coincidence, instead taking the old man's hand and kissing it appreciatively. "Thank you, Azim," she said before running off in the direction he had indicated.

"Slow down, girl," he called after her, "before the Watch takes you in for suspicion."

But Corine had barely heard him.

The street was strangely quiet, though sounds of merriment in the Kingdom tongue could be heard from within the two-story Inn of the *Speared Grahrk*. Corine approached cautiously, suddenly feeling as though she was being watched. The dusty square leading to the stone steps of the Inn were deserted, but the alleys surrounding it were shrouded in darkness and echoes. Corine glanced back at the harbor, seeing the masts poking out from behind the darkened buildings and the limp canvass and flags hanging in the still night. There was no breeze, only the stale air hanging like a curtain between her and the Inn where the *Goddess*'s crew was hopefully waiting.

With her first tentative step into the square Corine knew she was being observed. She turned her calm walk into a mad dash for the door of the *Speared Grahrk*. Ten steps across the open square and Corine was panting as though the very demons of Hell were on her tail. Within another five steps she was almost in tears, but she knew she only had another few paces to go. Within a foot of the door a figure in black had emerged from the darkness and clamped vice-like arms around her slim, quivering body. A second figure appeared from the other side of the Inn, trapping Corine's scream in a leather glove. The two men dragged her from the awning and into the shadows of the alley behind the house.

"Keep her quiet," a man said in disgust as Corine struggled and tried to scream again. This third figure was large and his voice familiar. He raised a lit match to study his capture, and Corine managed a good look at her captor, gasping when she recognized him. "Well, well," General Azel Tulambec, harbormaster of Shebwai said when he finally brought the light close enough to his prey. "The Kingdom serving girl. I never thought I would see *you* again. Still, it makes sense, given the men I seek this night." Corine tried to shake her head, to wriggle free, even to bite the hand that gagged her, but her captors were strong, armored, and experienced. "Indeed," he said as even more men appeared from the night and made for the door of the Inn. "They must be inside. Bring them to me," he smiled victoriously.

Corine tried to cry out one last time, but the punch to her ribs stole the very air from her lungs.

"When this is over," Azel whispered promisingly, "you will be the one I torture first."

The room was dark and full of smoke, but it was the drinking that had robbed James Jovark of much of his sight. He regarded the pitcher in his hand as though for the first time, then took another drink. "Where's Telorn?" he asked, carefully forming the words around his thick tongue.

Jack Kloot looked briefly at the other crewmen of the *Angry Goddess* seated at the table, some with whores in their laps while others studied their cards. After a moment the young wizard turned to his captain with a concerned smile. "He told you, cap'n; he went to find a place to piss. Are you all right? I don't remember the last time you had this much to drink."

James nodded. "I am fine," he answered succinctly, finding his head still swaying up and down even after he had thought he'd stopped the motion. He glanced at the door, judging the sight to be a sobering moment. "I'm still coherent enough to fight those bastards."

Men jumped to their feet and drew swords from scabbards and sashes, and women fell to the floor or ran screaming from the room as three men in black with scimitars and knives rushed in from the front door.

"Oh, shite!" James exclaimed as he flew from his chair and drew his rapier. "Are there six of them?"

"Three, cap'n," Jack tried to explain, drawing a vial from his robes. "Here, see?" He popped the cork from the vial and let the smoke and dust it emitted hit James in the face. The pirate captain spluttered and coughed, letting the spell clear his vision and mind a bit before trying to again ascertain the situation. By that point, one of his men was on the floor, another pair was engaging the Shebwai agents, and Jack Kloot was behind James trying to devise a spell.

"Shite," James repeated, and drove the point of his blade towards the first black figure he could find. The sword bit deep into the man, eliciting a scream from behind his mask before he fell.

Once concocted, Jack's spell flung out in the form of a cloudy pink mist. The closest Shebwai agent saw it coming before the spell was even cast, though, and was prepared. His free hand sprang up, fingers curved into some arcane symbol. The pink cloud turned into light the moment it struck his fingers, and James found himself on the floor, the spell turned back onto the defenders.

A set of boots were apparently pinning the captain's sword arm to the floor. "Where did you find the women you sold at the auction two weeks ago?" an agent said, his blade now quite definitely at James's throat.

"What women?" James managed.

"Kingdom vermin," the masked Shebwai agent hissed, reminding James of his predicament by driving his knifepoint into the skin of his throat. "You're a spy of Capriana."

"Like hell!"

"Then where'd you get the women?" the agent demanded.

James looked around. Jack was on his back, unconscious. The rest of the crew that had been with him were almost further-gone, menaced by the huge scimitar of the remaining agent. "Same place I found your mother," he answered with a grin, "But she was prettier back then, even for a Shebwai slut."

"Dog!" The masked agent cursed, turning his knife to James's shoulder long enough to stab him once before returning it to his throat. "You're a spy; you hooked up with the Kingdom Navy on your last trip and brought in the women to spy on us. Admit it!"

"Who wants to know?" James countered.

"Kill him," the other Shebwai man said, raising his own blade to finish off the crew. "We'll get the truth from the girl."

"Like hell you will." Telorn was standing at the door to the Inn, a bloodied sword in one hand and a bound and gagged blonde girl clinging to the other. "I've dealt with the others, and my men are on their way," he told the two agents. "I suggest you leave."

The two masked men glanced at each other before removing their blades from where they threatened captain and crew. "Leave Shebwai on the next tide or die," the first one warned as he backed towards the door. The pair stopped when Telorn didn't immediately step aside from the door, but left quickly when he did so with a grin.

"Are you all right, J.J.?" the first mate said, rushing to James's side. The girl at his arm was dressed in the skimpy clothes of a rich slave, though the garments were torn slightly. Telorn began cutting her bonds, and when he removed the gag, James finally recognized the serving girl, Corine.

"I'll live. See to the others." James rose on shaky legs and helped Jack Kloot to his feet. "We should leave."

"I heartily agree, cap'n," Jack groggily said.

"There's three more dead outside," Telorn told him, helping the wounded men to their feet. "I managed to surprise them when I saw the vermin sneaking in."

"You mean you didn't cause all of this by going after her?" James accused, though he could tell by Corine's smiling reaction that she was pleasantly surprised by the notion.

"J.J.," Telorn said in mock anguish, "is that any way to thank me?"

"Well then what brought this hell down upon us?" James asked, holding his spinning head.

"I think I can answer that," Corine ventured. "But you've got to get me out of Shebwai."

"Maybe," James said, stepping outside. "But let's finish this conversation back on the *Goddess*. We need to weigh our options."

"More likely we need to weigh anchor," Telorn informed him when they came upon the body of General Azel beside the Inn.

"Hell's teeth!" James spat. "Did you have to kill him?"

"He wouldn't stay down," Telorn shrugged. "And he threatened to kill Corine."

Turning to Corine James shook his head. "Where's Eronica? We need to be out of this city on the Moon tide."

"She's in the Sultan's Harem," she said, exasperated.

"Then there's nothing we can do," Telorn announced.

"We can't leave without her!" James told him.

Corine smiled at his obvious feelings. "Get us to Kingdom waters, captain. I'll do the rest—only then can we hope to rescue my mistress."

James rolled his eyes. Regarding his dead foe, he let out a long breath. "Hide the body and get Corine safely aboard. Tell the crew; we're not long for this city."

"Aye, cap'n."

Night had fallen and Eron still waited alone. The small chamber near the Harem was cold, featureless stone against her knees and closing in on her senses. She'd been left there for what felt like hours, guarded by two of the Sultan's men. Informed that she was awaiting punishment for her contact with the outside, the guards had come for her as the moment she had moved her meager belongings out of Sacha's room. Now Eron worried that Jatuu might somehow suspect something more, and the wait was the Sultan's deciding how best to kill her.

When the guards from Jatuu's room finally arrived with manacles in their hands, Eron was hardly surprised. She had often noticed the pair standing mute and indifferent within the Sultan's chambers, wearing only loincloths. She remained silent as one dressed her in a thin silk robe to cover her tiny harem costume. He held Eron's arms behind her while the other secured the cold irons to her wrists and helped her to stand. The two men, both stunning examples of chiseled desert youths, continued their resolute silence as they led her from the stone chamber.

Eron was stunned to now find herself standing before Jatuu in his throne room instead of his bed, a detail that scared her all the more. While no one else was in the chamber, it was a change in treatment that humbled Eron in ways that she could not completely hide in her expression. "Strip her," he commanded simply.

The two guards at her sides obeyed with enthused expediency. They grabbed at the thin robe they had just donned on her cold skin and tore the garment free. It came away easily but with a quiet ripping sound that added violence to the simple maneuver. Eron couldn't help but gasp as their hands again reached for her body and their hot, hard fingers hooked into the straps of her bodice and shorts and pulled. The cloth came free with a rending sound, the jerking movement pulling her to and fro, making Eron balance on her toes as best as possible. The act complete, one servant suddenly placed his vice-like grip on her bound arms and forced her to her knees. Then the two men were waved away, and Eron was left nude and panting at her master's mercy, a predicament that made Eron wet despite the terror it infused into to her very soul.

"What am I to do with you?" Jatuu asked, standing at last and walking around her prone form. He was clothed in turquoise silks and a pair of leather riding boots, his mood cold despite the desert heat. "You do not behave as Shebwai slaves do, and this excites me, I admit." From his belt he pulled forth a large leather flogger with a multitude of long, thick straps. He dangled it before her only a moment before stepping behind Eron and hitting her across the back and ass with a resounding crack that almost sent her off her knees and onto her side. She managed to hold back the tears, but the wetness coursed between her thighs of its own volition.

"But you do not listen to the rules that matter in my home, even venturing outside of its walls." He struck her with the giant flogger again. "This angers me."

"Master," Eron attempted, hoping to explain somehow that she was not the only one who had used the courtyard.

"You wish to speak?" He asked from behind her.

"Yes, Master."

The flogger struck her backside again, harder this time. "Too bad." Jatuu moved to stand before her and released his erect cock from the silken breeches. "Take me into your mouth," he commanded.

Eron had to maneuver herself over to him on her knees, an uneasy prospect with her hands bound behind her and her backside still smarting. She took his engorged phallus between her lips greedily, a part of her hoping to the Gods that she could somehow placate him if only to survive. Eron moaned around its girth each time he whipped her with the leather device.

Her head bobbed out and back. Eron let her hot, wet mouth work as a desperate diplomat trying anything to forego bloodshed. When the flogger slapped the length of her back again, she breathed a grunt of pain and want around his rod, then set to again. Eron's tongue tasted the sweet salt of the moment, knowing not if it was his juices or her own tears.

"Ohh, Eron," Jatuu groaned, "I cannot hate you for your transgression." He grunted, coming quickly and spilling his seed down her open throat. When he was finished coming, he smiled down and said, "You are entirely too vigorous a filly for that."

Jatuu stopped the beating, taking her chin between her fingers and allowing his cock to slide languorously out of her sticky mouth. "But you are a Kingdom woman," he said, looking down into her large eyes. "I should not have the feelings that I do."

Eron was uncertain of what to say. Just as more complicated issues were replacing the relief of not being somehow discovered as a spy, the doors to the throne hall opened with an echoing thud, startling them both out of the moment.

Hanim Krel's overbearing aura preceded him into the room. Jatuu adjusted his clothes, ignoring the necromancer's usual breech of protocol. "You've returned already?" he asked, smiling. "Is it done?"

"It is, Holiness," Krel responded in a pleased tone. "But not without expense."

Jatuu was suddenly alight with victorious glee. Waving Krel's portent away he said, "What matter? You are returned and your task is done!"

"But I have learned much," Krel warned again. "Come. To my chambers."

Again the Sultan forgot his wizard's lack of protocol and followed the giant black man from the room. He snapped his fingers once. "Come, Eron," Jatuu commanded.

She stood, still naked and bound as she hurried on bare feet to catch up with her master. Eron tried not to think of how humiliating her eagerness and fear made her now act. She needed to escape this place, she knew, and soon.

Azim was smoking his pipe, dangling his feet over the edge of the pier next to the *Angry Goddess*. He looked up when Captain James Jovark and the others approached out of the night. "You're coming home late," he chided with a smile.

James eyed the old foreman for a moment. "Azim; my boat does not need guarding."

"I thought you might try leaving," he answered with a shrug. "A foolish prospect, even on a night as dark as this."

James looked around him suspiciously, half expecting the dock's guards to come crashing down at any moment. But the air stayed still, and the stars did not crumble away. "How dangerous?" he asked at last.

Azim smiled and dumped his ashes into the sea. "I thought as much," he said, eyeing Telorn and the girl Corine. "If you can stick to the shallows on the west bank without beaching her, you'll avoid the night watch until it's too late for them to fire on you." He groaned as he stood up on bent legs. "There's talk that a Kingdom fleet is massing at the edge of Shebwai waters. Perhaps you'll reach them before one of the Sultan's warships can sink you."

"Perhaps," James smiled. He grabbed the foreman's arm before he could walk away. "Wait," he said, and handed him a purse of gold. "For your troubles."

Azim snorted, but took the purse. "My troubles begin when your Kingdom fleet arrives, I'm sure. Perhaps, though, it's time to cut my losses and leave this city. I've amassed enough money—if I hurry, I can pay for a decent caravan to take me to my daughter in the hills"

"Maybe I should ask for my money back."

"Bah!" Azim complained, waving him off, "nobody ever paid me for the damned repairs to your boat!"

"Azim!" James called, and tossed him another purse when he turned. "Go to your daughter. Be safe." He looked heavenward, adding with certainty, "War is coming."

Krel's chamber was across the courtyard from the Sultan's. Eron tried to make light of her bound, nude form as she was paraded throughout the palace on their way to the necromancer's apartments.

The rooms themselves were similar in size and layout to the Sultan's, but the air became chilled and still the moment they passed over the threshold. Some of the women of the harem, in their fear of the necromancer's mystery, had called him a butcher and the true power of Shebwai. Eron agreed with much of the assessment instantly upon entering his quarters.

The chamber walls were devoid of the color and decoration that painted every corner of the rest of the palace. Instead, these were blackened and charred, as though burned or scarred by whatever horrors Krel called forth with his magic each night. The stench led Eron's eyes to the corners, where tattered bones lay in piles beside glass vats of noxious chemicals. In one alcove, though, there was life—chained and naked, the bloodied forms of a man and a woman sat against the wall, silent yet breathing.

"These," Krel indicated with a dramatic wave of his massive arm. "These are the spies I have been seeking."

Eron's heart almost stopped. Here at last she had found the people who were supposed to have contacted her and helped her to eventually escape. Her pity for their own fate was only eclipsed by her fears that she was now truly trapped, and facing annihilation should they somehow betray her. Eron stiffened, looking away in sincere disgust while trying not to give away anything compromising.

"Between the last spy and the thoughts of the King himself, I was finally able to track down these two," Krel said proudly.

"Then it is truly done?" Jatuu asked triumphantly.

"It is," Krel said with a vicious smile. "My spell was perfect—no one suspected. King Henrick II is dead… thrown," he laughed, "from his own horse."

It was all Eron could do just to suppress her gasp of pain and shock or sink to her knees in horror. Dead. Her king—the only other one in her homeland to know where she was—Dead. It seemed impossible, but she knew that this monster somehow spoke the truth.

"Thrown from his horse," Jatuu exclaimed. "Amazing. How did you do it, Hanim?"

"With pleasure," Krel hissed, then broke into a terrible laughter, which Jatuu joined in on. The Sultan, a man Eron had become lover and slave to, was somehow partly to blame for the assassination of her beloved king. Now Jatuu didn't even seem to notice her presence in the room as they laughed over Henrick's death. Cold, frightened, and utterly alone, Eron wanted to wrap her arms about her nudity and shrink away. But Krel's cold, knowing eyes caught her where she stood and burned into her very soul. She could almost hear him in her mind, laughing, raking his mind over hers as though it were his hands having their way with her body.

Chapter 13

The sun's rays awoke her. The sky was bright and inviting through the windows of the Sultan's chambers, but Eron only felt cold and exposed. Jatuu's lovemaking had been hard and impersonal, tainted by a grin of faraway power on his once noble visage. She hated and pitied him now, as much for his part in the death of her king as his pathetic loss of humanity at the hands of a devil he believed to be his servant.

If nothing else, Eron had learned the truth behind the influence that drove the armies of Shebwai and their master. Hanim Krel held the true, evil powers of Shebwai in his powerful grip. She wished in quiet futility that she could help the Kingdom agents Krel held for torture, but Eron knew there was nothing that could be done for them. Their bloodied bodies had haunted her dreams.

She arose naked and raw from the bed. Before, Eron had hoped only to be at Jatuu's side somehow until the chance to escape came. Here, in these chambers at least and not in that bitchy harem, she had lived with the façade of warmth and power. Eron realized now that power was nothing. Her true desires lay on the sea—a love that she may never again be reunited with. She had hid her hate and rage from the necromancer she now so despised, just as she had held back the tears from the cold master she was still forced to serve. But she could not hide the truth from herself. She wanted desperately to leave and would have given anything, even her return home, to be back in the arms of James and his love.

"You loved him." It was the Sultan, awake at last.

Eron turned, uncertain and afraid of what he might mean. "Master?" she managed.

"Your king," Jatuu repeated. "You loved him?"

Eron swallowed her pride once more. "As any servant loves her king, Master." She accented the statement with a bow. "Nothing more."

The usually calm Sultan suddenly seethed with spite. "He was a fool and deserved death. So much of the world between his own kingdoms and the frontiers and wastes, and he claims it all as his own. Yet he would never lower himself to discuss my rights as his equal. He threw my generous attempts at negotiations back in my face, and now he has paid the price for his folly." Jatuu calmed at last, and turned away from Eron's shocked expression, but repeated, "He deserved death."

Eron wanted to argue with him, though she knew it was a useless gesture. Her honor and hurt could not remain completely silent, however. "Are you trying to convince me of that, Master?"

"You are mine," he claimed, "but you were a kingdom woman, once. You must understand why I do the things I must."

"I will never understand," she said coldly. "I thank the gods for that, at least."

"You think me cruel," he accused. "I am cruel. A Sultan must be when the time calls for it. But I am no monster." Jatuu stared at her, seemingly trying to decide whether to dismiss her as a foolish slave or continue the argument as though he cared what she thought of him. "Hanim Krel desires you for himself. If you wish to know the definition of cruelty, then run to his arms if you dare."

"I do not desire him," Eron said, once again proudly dispensing with the addition of 'Master' to her retort. "I guess I shall never know true cruelty."

Jatuu sneered as though stung. "Now you berate me for keeping such a man in my service. Once again, you go too far, Eron."

"And yet you do not send me away," she countered. "Why must I understand how your ways are somehow right while men die in battle and women serve in your Harem with no hope of becoming more than mere slaves of pleasure?"

"You wish for more?" he yelled back at her. "You are a favorite in the Harem of the Sultan of Shebwai. There is no higher station for a woman!"

Eron kept her voice calm and quiet. "Laurallin would wish for recognition of her place of power at your side. Sacha would wish to be Sultana, secure as your wife and yet free to see the sky. It is not enough for them to always be playthings to your whim."

Jatuu advanced on her, coming to tower over Eron who held her own ground. "And what of you? The Kingdom whore who greedily sucks my cock and pleasures both her master and herself with her wanton ways now wishes more than to be a simple plaything?"

"I am your slave," Eron told him succinctly. "I do what I must, and I enjoy pleasure. That does not mean it is all I want or am capable of." Her hand went to his arm carefully, calmly, stroking his bicep through the rich robe. "Jatuu, you have settled your debt of pride with Capriana's king. Turn back now before Hanim Krel's evil plans drag you down forever."

But the Sultan of Shebwai only stared back at her, removing her hand from his arm. "No slave commands me, and none ever shall." He turned away from her at last, dropping his robe and clapping for his servants to attend him. Instantly several women appeared and began to wrap his naked body in silks, dressing him in the clothes of his station. "Return to the Harem, Eron. When my navy has returned from sinking the Kingdom fleet to the bottom of the sea, perhaps I will again be in the mood to be entertained by such a willing whore."

Eron visibly blanched at his cold words and rejection of peace. She found a robe of her own and covered herself, ignoring the grinning eyes of the serving girls as they watched her pass by, departing their Master's chambers.

The sun had risen and James was pleased that the sea behind his vessel was devoid of the land of Shebwai or her ships.

"Heading, cap'n?" Telorn asked aloud.

"Damned if I know," James answered honestly. The idea of sailing headlong into the Capriana navy seemed foolish at best at this point. At worst, it sounded suicidal. He had little choice, though, and it might be the only chance for his crew's families now that Shebwai was forever behind them. He could never return there and be sure that he and his men wouldn't be implicated in General Azel's death. James could foolishly assume that he was still in the Sultan's employ, but that meant still serving a man who possessed the woman he loved. Returning to Kingdom waters was an equally dangerous prospect, as he was a hunted Pirate who had worked for the Sultan of Shebwai. The open sea stared back at James with disdain, leaving him with no idea where he stood in the world.

Corine was in the Mate's cabin, biting her nails nervously as she watched the sea from a window. "Captain," she greeted when he entered. "Telorn," she breathed, rushing into the first mate's arms when he followed James in.

"I'm sorry," Telorn told the relieved girl. "I had duties, but we can be together now, for a time."

"Thank you," she said genuinely. "You saved me last night, and I never got to ask why."

Telorn smiled sheepishly. "I couldn't stop thinking of you, I admit it."

"Nor I you," she laughed. "But we've no time for such things; Lady Eronica is in danger. We must make haste for the Kingdom ships the old man spoke of."

"Why?" James demanded.

"Sorry?" she stammered, having apparently forgotten that the pirate captain was standing there.

"Why?" he repeated. "Why must we give ourselves to the kingdom fleet like lambs to the slaughter?"

Corine heaved a sigh. "Because it's the only thing that will save Eron's life," she answered.

"And what do I learn from that?" he asked, finally at his wit's end.

Corine let out a breath. "You learn that she is a Kingdom Agent, sent by King Henrick into the arms of the Sultan as a spy to learn his true motives."

"*Eventually you are going to have to fight back or die,*" Eron had told James. Then she had added cryptically, "*I am going to set us free.*"

"Gods," James said in genuine amazement, and sat down on the edge of a chest. "Gods," He said again. "I can't believe it."

"Believe it," Corine told him. "She has no way out of that palace now except us, and we can't do it alone. But if I can convince the Kingdom fleet of our connection to Eron and her mission, we—and Eron—may have a fighting chance."

James was silent another moment before he finally looked at Corine, seeing her in a new light. "You're an amazing pair, you know that."

"I hope so, captain," she said.

Nodding resolutely to himself, James left the couple to their romance and made for the command deck. "Jack Kloot!" he called to his resident spell-caster.

"Aye, Cap'n?" Jack called from the crow's nest.

"Time for you to employ the tools of your trade, man." James called out so that the entire crew could hear. "Use your abilities and search the seas to the north. Find us the Kingdom navy and set sail. We're going home!"

A day had passed, and Eron was still just as miserable. The hot days in the Harem were listless and boring, and she refused to eat much more than a handful of food or drink more than some simple water. The other girls whispered amongst themselves of her fall from grace, and few gave her what could be called a kind look. Instead they giggled and quit her company en masse to spend time in the pool or smoke the hookah amongst the cushioned parlor rooms. Eron ignored them, thinking only of a home she would never see and a captain she had come to love too late. She hoped that at least Corine might have found peace somewhere, perhaps even back aboard the *Goddess*.

Taking a deep breath, the Kingdom Lady decided that this was a useless way to spend another day. She could start to look for an escape from the palace. She would have to be stealthy, and it might take weeks, but starting now Eron was determined to escape with what she had learned for her Kingdom and somehow—anyhow—get back home. She stood, proud and erect, ready to take on whatever came her way. *Perhaps*, she thought, *I can still fool Jatuu and get back into his good graces long enough to find a way out.* On the other hand, the further she was from the Sultan, the less often she might run into Hanim Krel. She looked up through a skylight, determined to be under that hot sun and out of the city within a month. The Kingdom of Capriana would have to take care of itself until then.

Eron padded down the hall in her bare feet and found the dressing rooms devoid of Harem girls and most of the servants. There was one aging woman who silently helped her dig some simple clothes from a chest and brushed Eron's hair as she put on an uncomplicated necklace of pearls. She left the usual coins and jewels aside, not wanting their jangling to attract attention. Her belly chain and earrings were the only gold she wore. Eron then bound her ample chest in a tiny, embroidered bodice with a plunging, rounded neckline that made her breasts jiggle with each small step. Slipping into a billowing, almost sheer pair of satin pantaloons, Eron stepped into the darkness of the halls of the Harem leading to the rest of the palace.

She spent the morning searching the walls and tapestries for any hidden doors that may be secreted in the palace. Capriana's castles were replete with such oddities, constructed over the centuries by Lords and Ladies of every station who wished to secretly rendezvous with some other party whenever they desired. A castle devoid of a secret tunnel was practically an oddity in her land, but here Eron could find no such channel. Shebwai's secrets guarded themselves, and leaving the Harem unnoticed seemed impossible for a girl of her station.

When she saw that many of the servants were congregating for lunch, Eron thought it was time to return to the center of the Harem or possibly be missed. She stayed in the less-frequented halls and passed noiselessly back towards the rooms she shared with the others. She could hear the laughter of the women and the false safety of the Harem's shelter when she stopped dead in her tracks.

Once again the giant black shape of Hanim Krel confronted her, barring her way forward. "It is time, Lady Eronica of Tibeth." His bearded visage split into a wide grin, but there was nothing warm in the gesture.

"You can't be here," Eron stammered, trying to avert his gaze and ignore his knowledge of her true name and title. "I'll scream for the guards."

"Time for truth between us," he continued, ignoring her threat. Krel's deep voice became low and menacing. "The Sultan is busy overseeing the battle raging at sea, and he will not miss you now. Come." His arm seemed to reach for her, only to sweep aside in an arc of glowing power and clouds of evil, gray smoke. The smoke reached for her like tendrils of seaweed, grasping her limbs and forming into chains. The cloud darkened and Eron watched the space around her change from the Harem halls into the chamber of the Necromancer.

Eron screamed, but the sound was only an echo in the still, empty hall of the Harem.

The sea was a deafening storm of war. The cacophony had started the moment that the *Angry Goddess* had sighted the Kingdom fleet the day before, already engaged in battle with the warships of Shebwai. The order to turn the *Goddess*'s canons on the ships of those desert rats had been a glorious moment in James's life, and the roar in his ears had hardly abated since. His vessel had navigated its way through the graveyard of sinking ships and floating men, on through the shattered lines to either join the ranks of the Kingdom, or be sunk then and there as traitors. What had happened next had surprised even Captain James Jovark.

No sooner had the crew caught sight of the magnificent splendor of the Capriana flagship, when suddenly the *Goddess*'s deck was full of Kingdom soldiers and their imposing commanders, transported there by the magic of the King's own wizard. The tense moment came when all were ordered to lay down their arms, and James had been left hoping that sinking two Shebwai ships on the way in had paved the way for good communication at the very least.

A general, the wizard, and another elegantly dressed officer wearing a helm of white plumage had stood before James, demanding he swear allegiance and state the business of the *Angry Goddess* and her crew.

"I come to lead the way to Shebwai harbor," James had said. "The Sultan's army stands ready to march once more, and an agent of your king is held captive in the Sultan's harem."

"Does he speak the truth?" the kingdom general had asked of his richly dressed wizard.

"He does," Corine had said, interrupting the interrogation and coming to stand before the helmed officer to fall upon her knees. "I beg audience with my Prince."

"You recognize me?" Prince Henrick III smirked, removing his helm.

"How could I not?" Corine smiled, standing. "Though I am surprised to find you with the King's navy, Highness."

"The King has been assassinated," the general interjected, "and telling the Prince where he must stay has been the impossible task of the past few days."

Corine's hands flew to her mouth. "The King is dead?"

Henrick III helped her to stand, smiling sadly. "Shebwai's spells tried to make it look like an accident, but the royal magicians can track such deceptions. I've come to stop this madness, now." He had turned to James, his smile fading. "And what of you, pirate? What agent of my father's do you speak of?"

"The Lady Eronica."

Henrick looked to Corrine with renewed concern. "Is this true?"

"It is, Highness," she answered. "Your father's mission was secret, but she was sent there to spy on the Sultan, and now she cannot escape."

"They speak the truth, highness," the royal wizard intoned. "And I sense more; grave and deadly magicks are being woven around us as we speak. I know not what powers are being gathered, but I suspect the Sultan's necromancer is drawing the darkness against us. We should return to the flagship and make haste to Shebwai and stop them."

"Very well," Henrick III had said, covering his noble visage with his helm. "Join the ranks of our fleet, pirate—you're part of Capriana's navy, now."

And so the armada had sailed for Shebwai and battle, with the *Angry Goddess* among the front ranks to cross into Shebwai harbor. Now Captain James Jovark looked at the home fleet and defending forces of the Sultan himself, their canons spewing fire at the waterline of his beloved ship.

The largest company of men James had ever had under his command filled his deck and snarled at their onrushing enemies, then brandished their swords as they came within boarding range of another Shebwai ship. The sea boiled and exploded into the sky as the Royal Magicians fired a volley of whatever spells they had concocted directly into the foredeck of the Shebwai flagship. The curved timbers and polished metals of the enemy vessel splintered into a million pieces, sending men to their watery graves. The way ahead to the harbor cleared away as the ships of the Sultan slipped into the bubbling, churning waves.

"A bag of gold to the first man to reach the Palace," James challenged as the *Goddess* closed on the harbor. "Death to the Sultan!"

A cheer went up from sailor and soldier alike, and James looked back at the open sea one last time, praying that all might survive long enough to even reach the Sultan's gates.

Do you hear that?" Hanim Krel asked her. The dull thuds of canons firing from far beyond the palace could be heard, even through the darkened rocks that made up the necromancer's chambers. "My plans have advanced faster than I anticipated. Those dullard Royal Magicians must have followed my trail better than I gave them credit for."

"What are you talking about, madman?" Eron hung limply in a set of shackles set into the grimy wall. Dazed from the spell that had brought her there, she'd put up no fight when Krel bound her there and left her to attend to his own devices. Torches burning some noxious, evil concoction were set next to her, sweating away what little energy and resolve fear had not already robbed from her. Even after hours of hanging there silently, Eron managed to glare at him through the wet strands of her hair and muster a strong voice to oppose him. "What trail?"

"The spell I used to kill your king, of course, spy." He was looking right at her with those piercing eyes again. Once more, shock and hatred of this man fired Eron's will. Hanim Krel was imposing and powerful, perhaps even attractive under better circumstances; but he was evil incarnate, and she was determined to fight him with her last breath.

His face, chiseled and bearded, was a gleaming handsomeness of black skin beneath the dull black robe. Krel turned from her to remove his belt of potions and pouches, and set fire to a large metallic brazier in the center of his room. The powders within the steel pit ignited and the room exploded into colors and smoke that danced along the walls and the folds of the necromancer's robe. He loosed the sash of his flowing garment and let it fall, revealing a form of physical perfection clad only in a loincloth. Krel's body—like his face—was a chiseled, molded sight one could only behold and admire, cast in gleaming obsidian and peppered with black hair. A full, muscular chest and wide, rounded shoulders tapered down to narrow hips, sculpted abs and thighs of chorded tissue. He pulled once at his beard as he regarded her in her tiny dancing costume, then ran a hand over his own chest as he contemplated her future. "I've suspected you for some time— I'm glad I was right and I finally get to entertain you personally."

"You bastard," Eron managed.

"You have no idea," he said with a chuckle. "I tried to make Henrick's death look like an accident. I had hoped that the Sultan would be able to conquer more of the Five Kingdoms before things came to a head. But the King's son is here to settle the score, and I must make the most of what I have wrought."

Eron's head turned as the sounds of war crept closer to the palace, sparking the tiniest hope that somehow she might be rescued. "The Kingdom navy? You're going to just let them come here?"

"I have work to do," he shrugged. "Perhaps you'll survive long enough to see what will happen when your beloved Prince's army comes through that door, but I doubt it. The spell I'm preparing requires…" Krel paused, raking his eyes over Eron's sweat-soaked body. "Requires the deepest of magicks, and that only comes from the truest, most basic carnal pleasures."

Eron stifled a shiver that trickled down her spine like a chilled bead of sweat. She knew he meant to rape and murder her.

The doors to the Sultan's room swung open, and Jatuu and his honor guard marched into the room. He was dressed in a flowing silk uniform, a giant curved sword at his side and a jeweled, feathered turban on his head.

"You could not see this coming?" the Sultan demanded. The enemy is at my very gates and here you sit, conjuring smoke!"

Hanim Krel made a dismissive gesture. "I am sorry, Holiness—our plan has backfired, and the Prince has come to avenge his dead father. I can do nothing; my arts are held in check by whatever powers the Kingdom magicians bring against us."

"He's lying, Jatuu," Eron called out. "Don't listen to him!"

The Sultan at last noticed where Eron hung from her chains, and she briefly hoped against hope that somehow he might release her and come to his senses. "What is this?" he demanded of his necromancer. "You have taken a member of my harem without my permission—I should kill you for these dishonors!"

Krel lifted one hand, his will and countenance alone stopping the guards before they could even move against him. "Hold, my Sultan. This woman is a Kingdom spy."

Desperately Eron's eyes pleaded her former lover's. "Jatuu! Please, he is mad."

"I speak the truth," Krel said evenly. "I might be able to break the spells put against me by using her, but only if given time."

Jatuu Olumbai, Sultan of Shebwai, regarded the woman he had held in such high regard with hurt eyes. When another explosion, closer this time, sounded outside, his face returned to a mask of rage. "Do as you will with her," he said finally, then turned and left, slamming the doors behind him.

Krel's face split into a grin, and he turned back to regard Eron who had been left trembling in her bonds. "Oh, I shall."

Smoke filled the air and the sounds of charging troops and screaming death filled James's ears. His rapier sang out, carving his way from the docks to the streets. For the hundredth time he looked up at the Palace atop the hill, gleaming in the light despite the black clouds threatening to envelope everything. James hung back as another squad of Kingdom troops pushed forward, charging the Shebwai scimitars with courageous abandon. He and some of his crew had gone ashore with the first waves, hoping to catch some of the glory or looting or both. Only Eron's raven hair filled James's mind, though, and he waited impatiently for the clear to sound so that he could rush up the next street and be that much closer to her before he might be felled by a sharp blade or a magician's blast.

"I'm coming, Eron," he said as he ran blindly into the smoke. "Hold on—whatever it takes, just hold on."

Krel reached out and fastened a leash to Eron's collar, once again reminding her of her station since reaching Shebwai. His imposing, near-naked body was close to her, towering and hot. "*Renich tolsham,*" he intoned, snapping his fingers to ignite the spell he was casting over her. A thin wisp of blue smoke crackled from between his thumb and finger as though there had been a match held there, and Eron's sharp gasp at the action only served to breathe the spell directly into her nostrils. She coughed and tried to exhale, but it was too late. Already exhausted, she slumped in her chains as the glamour turned her muscles into traitors.

Krel easily removed the chains from the shackles of her ankles and wrists, picking Eron up bodily in his hot hands and pulling her against his large chest to drag her over to a place on the floor near the smoking brazier. He laid her face down, fastening chains set in the flagstones to her wrists and the leash at her neck. She panted, panicking as her senses began to heighten while her will remained submissive. *My Gods*, Eron thought, *what has he done to me?*

"On your knees," he commanded, and Eron's body obeyed, groggily getting up onto all fours and spreading her knees to allow the necromancer to secure her ankles to similar short chains. She was left in the basest form of supplication, swaying as her head swam from whatever draft he'd infected her with. "The Sultan has been easy to control with sluts like you and Laurallin around to distract him, I must admit. It has let me get on with my own work. Now that the King is dead, I can finally do as I wish to you, and with the Prince here, I'll have every pleasure I have dreamed of soon at my disposal."

Eron could feel the necromancer's spells washing over like her like a faintly blown mist from the sea. A drunken warmth accompanied the sensations, along with the prickling knowledge that the glamour was changing her body's reactions. A sheen of sweat covered Eron's body, like a wave had crashed over her all but naked body. She flung the soaking rivulets of her dark hair over her shoulders, causing strands to stick to her face and neck. Eron tried to ignore the strange feeling overcoming her mind and body, putting it aside as best she could by somehow finishing her task and understanding this monster. "W-what pleasures?" she stammered.

"Anarchy, of course." Krel picked something up from beside the brazier and began to circle her. "Kings, Sultans, Lords and Marjahs, they are fools all. They seek to control men or to seize nature, and they think they can dictate *my* arts to do it. For decades I've watched their pathetic games play over and over. First father and then son, each tries to rule or conquer, dictating the law to their 'subjects' or crush a path through any natural resistance. They have all thought that they could control me—to use my kind or me. Finally, I'll show them all what hubris they conceive. King Henrick the First, the Sultan—each tried to use me, but now I'll show them all true power."

"Henrick the First?" Eron shook her head, confused. "But that would make you…"

"Almost a hundred years old," He finished, coming to stand behind her. "Kill enough youth and you retain your age, and I have killed many."

"Then all of this is revenge?" Eron asked in exasperation.

"Revenge, a cleansing of the old ways, returning disorder to an archaic, stifled, 'ordered' world—call it what you will. Whatever you label it, just know that the spell I wring from your flesh this day will destroy the Prince, the Sultan, and their armies in one act of devastation." She could hear the laughter of madness in his voice as he came to lean over her bare back.

Krel's short beard brushed her shoulder. "I've wanted you for some time, Eron. I just didn't want to give it away until I knew your purpose here and if you had contacts," he whispered into her ear. Each hissed word took her closer and closer to a desire she wanted desperately to deny, but the spell was settling in with a terrible vengeance. Eron could feel his erection though his silken loincloth nudging between her buttocks. Worse, she could feel a knife in his hand, threatening to scrape her bare skin. It only furthered her fear and excitement. He wanted her to enjoy anything he did to her, even while being aware enough to hate him for it. "You feel it, Eron?" he continued. "You feel it coming? I could torture you with need for days or kill you with pure pleasure within minutes.

The knife slipped under the fabric of her bodice, and Eron felt him make short work of cutting the garment into pieces. Her breasts hung free as the destroyed corset was pulled away. Eron moaned, trying desperately to control her fear.

"I want you to beg me for it," Krel was saying against her earlobe. His fingers found her swollen mound, wet and full against the thin material of her pantaloons. Just a tender stroke of his fingertips was enough to set her on fire. Eron felt his blade knick her shoulder and she gasped in pain, even though her body craved more. Krel's breath was hot against her face, tickling the hair stuck to her hypersensitive skin.

She shivered involuntarily at his oncoming tortures, left helpless in that humiliating position, subject to his every whim. Her head hung limp, and Eron watched as rivulets of sweat dripped from her face and hair to the stones beneath her. "H-how did you kill King Henrick?" she asked. "Leagues away and with his own necromancers close at hand; how?"

She felt him laugh against her naked back. He licked her spine once, causing her to shudder in a combined revulsion of the mind and enticement of the body. Then he was gone, walking back towards the brazier to stoke the fires and ingredients within. "I'll show you," he said at last. Krel tugged at his loincloth and it came undone, discarded to the floor.

He stood naked, bathed in the dancing lights of the spell-cauldron. She looked up at him, her eyes drawn to his penis. Krel's rod was thick and long even as it hung flaccid between his legs. Eron stared intently at it, willing her mind to want him as her body already craved, hoping that somehow that might allow her to survive whatever he did to her while his spells and sex-magicks worked their havoc on her body.

When he picked up a whip, Eron became certain of just what he intended to wrought upon her flesh. "*I can survive this,*" she whispered breathlessly to her own mind. "*Whatever tortures he inflicts, I can endure.*"

Krel smiled, as though he had heard her prayer and was determined to deny it. "King Henrick was thrown from his horse and broke his neck," he began to explain, tracing arcane symbols in the air over the fiery brazier. "Well, he thought it was his horse, but I switched myself for the animal once he was outside the protection of his palace." He took a drink from a vial and returned to his story. "I have mastered many arts, Eron. Teleportation, youth, and—most importantly—shape-shifting."

Krel's muscular thighs thickened, expanding and changing before Eron's eyes. She watched, the very breath stolen from her gaping mouth, as the bones and form of Hanim Krel's lower torso and legs all began to shift, bend, crack, and reassemble under the skin. A second set of legs protruded while his hindquarters extended and became a lengthened body; all the while Krel's chest and arms remained unchanged while he smiled with an evil glare. Soon it was not a man that stood before Eron, but a centaur—a beast of a horse's body and the torso of a man at the forefront.

The man-beast paced where he stood, still holding the whip in one perfect, human arm. Eron studied the centaur, admiring the creature's lines as if he were simply a horse—only this was a dangerous man in the guise of a beast, planning to take her like an animal and impale her on a giant, throbbing cock that even now stood erect and protruding under the belly of the beast. "Gods." She could not take her eyes off of its enormous length or terrifying girth. Eron knew she was lost—surely such a member would split her in two, if the glamour separating her mind from her soul didn't do it first. All the while the thought of him fucking her with that beastly thing drove her body mad with desire, sending a wetness coursing down the inside of Eron's thigh and a wanton trembling to her exhausted limbs and quivering muscles. She only hoped that her body's unbidden, traitorous desire would be enough to withstand the onslaught of the Centaur Krel's phallus.

Krel nodded, advancing on her. "It was in the horse's form that I killed your king. It is only fitting that I use this to fuck you to death and complete my spell. Enjoy this, Eron—it will be the last thing you ever experience."

The city had been taken by surprise. Half of the Shebwai army must have been a day's march out, James realized, for the next thing he knew, he and Telorn were storming the gates of the Sultan's Palace itself. They stood aside as a legion of Kingdom soldiers charged in and killed the first wave of palace defenders, then ran in after them alongside the Prince's personal magician. The servants cowered or ran, and the guards and defenders died. James and the invaders rushed up each set of steps and secured each chamber, killing any resistance with each room they took.

"Eron," James called to a scattering group of civilians. "Eron!"

Suddenly they were everywhere; the last line of defense was the Sultan's personal guard, a hundred strong. Armored men whittled down the King's army as they tried to funnel in through the chamber doors. James tried to find a way around, hoping to discover Eron still alive in the process.

He looked up, seeing the bells for the servants' chime and the ropes attached. They snaked up into the ceiling's hidden compartment, giving James an idea. Leaping, he grasped the ropes and climbed to the high ceiling, trying not to look down as men fought and died beneath him. James strained, his muscles bilging, fighting to keep the weight of his body and weapons aloft. His feet kicked out, and he scrambled into the tight compartment where the bell-ropes that ran into the adjoining chamber where housed.

It only took Telorn a moment's cursing to follow him up.

James was lost in the dark tunnel above the fighting, so he forged ahead, crawling until he reached the end, grinding his teeth all the way. He kicked the paneling out from under him when he could see down into the next room. James jumped the entire distance, gasping when his ankle twisted. He had landed behind the Shebwai defenders, just as he predicted, their attention so focused on guarding the doors that they didn't notice his entry.

James turned in time to see a man in a jeweled turban fleeing the room in the opposite direction. Telorn hit the ground beside him in time to engage the Sultan's two guards as they engaged to cover their master's escape. James slipped through the fight, his attention solely on his hated foe.

"Sultan!" he challenged, drawing his rapier. "Give me the Lady Eron and I'll spare your life."

Sultan Jatuu Olumbai turned, brandishing a large scimitar. The blade struck quick and fierce, all but knocking James's rapier away. The battle was joined.

Eron was trapped. Bound to the floor by chain on hands and knees, she could do nothing but give in to the pleasures of the flesh. Krel's whip lashed out, striking her back and pantaloons. The thin fabric tore, falling aside somewhat, allowing the air to wash across exposed skin. Eron cried out as the whip cracked again, tearing more of the garment and pulling most of it down her sweaty thighs. "Ungh," she moaned. "Ooh, Gods." The whip cracked again.

'It's alright, Eron.' Eron could hear Corine's voice in her mind. She opened her eyes, and Corine was kneeling naked before her. 'Give in,' she said, and caressed Eron's body with soft, ghostly hands before kissing her and licking her throat.

Then Krel Centaur was over her, positioning himself to have her. His forelegs knelt on either side of her, his horse-belly sliding across the smarting, whipped globes of her up-thrust ass. Krel's human hands reached down, entwining in her sweaty hair, caressing her fevered face. One giant finger snaked into her mouth. Eron's mind screamed *BITE*, but she hadn't the strength or will. Instead her tongue reciprocated the invasion and her mouth naturally suckled the digit, as though it was the manhood of her beloved James himself. '*Take it, Eron.*' A naked James, as ghostly an apparition as Corine had been, knelt before Eron's reddened face and offered himself to her. '*Take it.*'

"Aah!" Eron cried. Krel's cock slid between her thighs, tearing through the remaining cloth stretched across that barred his way. The phallus was like a chorded arm, curving up to rub her flat stomach and swollen mound and slide back and forth. Eron's heightened senses felt every inch of it snake across her quivering inner thighs, pressing up to grind her clitoris.

Nearby the strange coupling, the brazier of black magic flared.

"Gods, please," she begged.

"Gods, what?" he demanded, yanking on her hair so that she was forced to look up at him as he claimed her. "Say it. Beg for it." The giant cock slid tortuously slow along her slick channel, spreading the soaking lips wide.

"Don't stop," Eron whimpered, all reason and control gone. "I-I don't care if it kills me—just don't stop! It's amazing!"

Krel quickened his pace, grating his cock against her quim, legs, and belly; moving faster, increasing friction, but never quite penetrating her. He lashed down with his whip, curling the end as it struck so that it struck her swinging breasts and stung her hardened nipples.

"YES!" Eron came, her thighs locked upright in a violent tremor as her juices poured from her exposed pussy, over his thick phallus and down her legs. "Gods, fuck me! Fuck me!"

The brazier exploded in a shower of sparks.

The Krel-centaur snorted and laughed. "The spell is almost complete," he announced, pleased. "When I will it, you will die, and the palace will explode; at last, we shall all be free!"

His giant thighs shook and repositioned slightly, drawing back enough to bring the fist-like tip of his monster cock to her waiting pussy. "Where would you like it, whore?" he teased. "Here," and he shifted slightly, pressing the slimy tip to her most secret place. "Or here?"

Eron tried to look back, to see herself reveling in the ferocious carnality of the moment. Through the haze of the glamour and her tears and hair she could make out her shapely body, splayed out and willing, waiting to be impaled on his massive spike.

The lash wrapped itself around her ribs again. "Beg!" He whipped her again, striking her swaying breasts, making her scream. "Beg!"

"Do it!" Eron commanded. "I want you! I want you inside of me!"

Krel's tip slid into her slick pussy, slowly opening her. The coals of black magic spit and hissed. Eron thought of her Love.

"Fuck me!" Eron half-gasped, her want so great. Tears coursed down her hot cheeks, the visions of her love shimmering, replaced by hot lust.

The whip cracked.

Eron groaned, tossing her hair, but Krel grasped it and held her still as he slid the head into her, whipping her breasts again. She thought of her friend, Corrine, and how she would never again see her.

The coals became a flame.

The cock slid another inch into her, splitting Eron. She screamed in a hoarse cry of pleasure gone mad. James's image faded away forever, but the pleasure remained, spilling over. She had to feel it in her, even if it killed her.

The fiery brazier erupted, spilling a sulfurous gas into the air.

Mere inches from falling headlong over the edge to climax, Eron pulled away from the abyss. She rocked forward, sliding off of Krel before he could complete his painful thrust into her. Slumping aside as best she could, Eron squeezed her eyes shut, knowing she could never truly escape, but free of the glamour at last.

"NO!" she cried, broken but finally defiant and in control. She gasped, her muscles failing her as her cry tore the final breath from her strained lungs.

The doors flew open, and Jatuu suddenly backed in, his scimitar flashing in the torchlight as James struck out with his own sword, hacking away with the strength of ten.

JAMES!

"Fools!" Krel dismounted Eron, rearing back in rage at the intrusion before the spell could be irrevocably finished. The centaur backed away from the duel, and Krel's voice bellowed in hate. "I shall kill you all!"

"James!" Eron cried aloud. She smiled and sobbed in release as much as open disbelief. The unquenchable desire to die under the necromancer's lash and sex melted away. The spell was broken. Eron's chains dissolved into filmy smoke, leaving her bound only by the leash tethered to the floor. Her limbs were barely even able to support her weight, but Eron held herself on one shaky arm long enough to free the leash. She collapsed to the warm stones, her chest heaving from the ordeal.

James's attention was solely on the duel at hand. Several small cuts had caused blood to seep through his billowing shirt and tights, staining his sash and flared boots. He had chanced one glance, letting slip a tiny smile at the sight of his beloved still alive, but it had almost cost James his life. His speed and agility with the rapier was barely enough to hold off the giant blade of Jatuu's scimitar.

James didn't even notice that the Krel-centaur was circling around behind him with a long pike, ready to skewer him in the back.

Eron rolled from her exhausted position and onto her feet. Ignoring her shaking legs, she stood proud, naked and strong. She whipped her sweat-plastered hair from her face and eyes and chanced her last steps towards the fiery brazier before all her ability to stand might melt away. With all the will she had left, Eron heaved her frail weight against the steel legs holding the brazier upright, pushing it towards the Necromancer, even as he drew back to cast his pike.

"Krel!" She screamed.

The brazier toppled, sending glowing embers and a terrific amount of blackened smoke crashing across the cobblestones. Coals flew out of the kettle, striking Krel across his back and his human shoulders.

Krel howled in pain and rage, but it was too late—the magically infused blaze smashed against his skin and horse's mane, catching fire and exploding into a charged Power. Light and smoke coalesced around the evil wizard, dissolving him away before Eron's eyes. In a moment, he was gone.

Jatuu took the distracting moment to jab at James with the tip of his mighty blade, but the pirate captain saw it coming. James stepped aside, letting the Sultan in close enough to rake the edge of his sword up Jatuu's gut and ribs. Jatuu screamed and crumpled to the floor, his sword clanging across the charred stones. James reversed his rapier quickly and dispatched him with the sword-point, ending the Sultan of Shebwai's brief suffering.

After a shocked moment of breathlessness, Jatuu Olumbai was dead.

"James," Eron called out from where she lay. "James, is it really you?"

Dropping his sword, James ran to her, scooping her prone form into his arms. "Eronica, you're alive!" His hands were firm on her naked body, cradling her, but one finger gently pulled the hair from her forehead and eyes. "Gods, are you alright?"

"I am now," she admitted.

"Please, you've got to be alright," James said, begging the gods to make it true. "I love you, Eron. I love you."

"I'm alright, my love," she smiled, tracing his bearded jaw with a fingertip and craning her neck to touch him with her lips. "I told you I would set us free."

James smiled, seeing the truth of it in her resolve. He leaned down, kissing her tender lips. Eron's strength returned, infused by his kiss. Her arms snaked around his neck, drawing him to her so that their tongues could entwine once more.

Telorn walked in, blood dripping from his sword and a wound in his shoulder. "Oh, good," he smiled. "That's over with."

Epilogue

James's grip on Eron's waist was strong and comforting. They stood side by side on the deck of the *Angry Goddess*, anchored in Shebwai harbor. Eron was dressed in a gown again, the slave's collar of Shebwai finally—and happily—discarded, replaced by an ornate choker of pearls from the Sea of Blue Longing. Still in a foreign land, Eron felt that she was home at last aboard the ship of her captain.

James had donned his best coat and shirt, pulling back his unruly black hair into a ponytail and smiling as he and his Lady stood before Prince Henrick III of Capriana.

"Captain James Jovark, I grant you and your crew their freedom," Henrick said, handing the wax-bound scrolls that made it official to the former pirate.

James reluctantly released Eron's hand and took the scroll, nodding happily. "Thank you, highness."

"It's the least I could do," Henrick shrugged. "Word will be sent forth from Shebwai to the governors of the lower Kingdoms that had been conquered—the Sultan is dead and Shebwai's power broken. I will grant them clemency if they quit their posts now, return to Shebwai, and never again harm another Kingdom citizen. Your crew's families will be safe," the Prince said resolutely, "I promise you."

James smiled, evidently pleased. "That is all I could ask, Highness."

Henrick nodded, turning to Eron. "And what of you, Lady Eronica of Tibeth? What did my father promise you in return for your secret mission?"

Eron squeezed James's hand before curtseying. "Your highness, our King's plans died with him. The land is at peace and I can return home. I ask nothing, save to take this free man as husband, if he'll have me."

"Eron?" James asked, cocking one eyebrow at her and smiling rakishly. "Truly?" When she nodded emphatically, he swept her up, dancing her in circles. "Well I won't have it," he laughed. "You'll just have to be content letting me take you as *my* wife!"

The Prince smiled warmly. "Well then I shall have to give you both suitable titles and lands. Something near the Ocean, I suppose; a man of the sea will have to be close to home, and a woman of the Kingdom won't be happy unless she is close to the court."

"I am certain we shall find a balance, highness," Eron answered once James was finished flinging her about the deck.

"Good. When we return, we shall find you estates that befit heroes of the Kingdom." The Prince gestured towards Corrine, coming to stand before the serving girl and the *Goddess*'s First Mate, Telorn. "And what of you, Corine— you could always come to the palace and become my... servant."

Corine and Telorn bowed. "Thank you, highness," she answered. "But I think Eron will need a hand at her new estates. Besides, I cannot deny the man that saved my life," she said, indicating Telorn.

"Fair enough," the Prince said. "Serve Eron well, but I expect to see you and your lover at Court in whatever new clothes your not-inconsiderable reward might buy you both."

Telorn and Corrine grinned at each other. "Yes, highness," they answered.

Eron and Corrine embraced blissfully. "Eron, it's so wonderful."

"I know, and I want you to be Maid of Honor," Eron said, holding her friend tight. "Thank you Corine—I owe you my life."

"Captain, you may set sail whenever you wish," Henrick announced. "I have business here, but you may head for home, papers in hand. I expect to see you in my palace in a month's time." He added with a twinkle in his eye, "and I expect an invitation to the wedding."

The pirates turned Lords regarded each other. "Well, J.J., what of it," Telorn said, shaking his captain's hand. "Think you can stand living in Capriana?"

James looked around, pretending the matter was private. "Don't tell anyone, mate, but yeah, I think I can cope with the hand that's just been dealt to me."

Eron wrapped one arm around her new fiancé, and they both looked out onto the horizon as the sun set over the vast ocean ahead. "Adventure?" she asked him.

"Oh yes," James nodded. "If I'm to brave Capriana's courtesans at your side then you must brave the sea at mine."

"We'll do it together," she agreed, resting her head against the leather sleeve of his coat. "I know life will never be boring with you, James. I love you"

"And I you," he said. "Never thought I'd utter that one again, but then you just revel in proving me wrong, don't you?"

"Aye, Cap'n," Eron laughed. "Now get your hide in that cabin and me out of these gowns—'tis no way for a pirate's wife to be seen in public!"

Author's Note

Thank you for buying this book. If you enjoyed *Eronica Unbound*, please help spread the word, by leaving a review on Amazon.com. Reviews don't need to be long to be effective: just say that you liked the story and why. You can also post reviews on Barnesandnoble.com and on Goodreads.com. Finally, you can tell people you know, in person, about the book, and encourage them to buy it, if they enjoy erotic stories.

About the Author

Scarlett Vaughn is an erotica author who lives with a cat.

HERO LORE

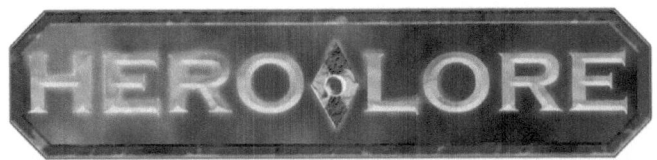

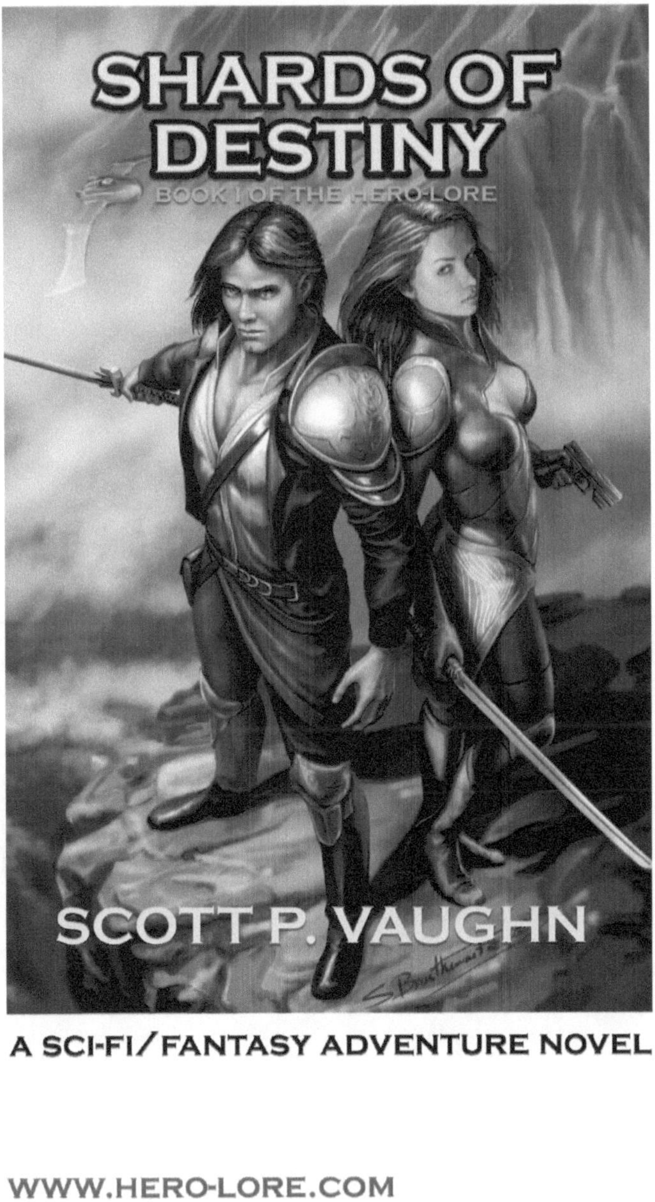
SHARDS OF DESTINY
BOOK I OF THE HERO-LORE
SCOTT P. VAUGHN

A SCI-FI/FANTASY ADVENTURE NOVEL

WWW.HERO-LORE.COM
WWW.VAUGHN-MEDIA.COM

WARBIRDS OF MARS

STORIES OF THE FIGHT!

SEAN ELLIS

RON FORTIER

STEPHEN M. IRWIN

J. H. IVANOV

DAVID LINDBLAD

JEFFREY J. MARIOTTE

ALEX NESS

CHRIS SAMSON

MEGAN E. VAUGHN

AND MORE

EDITED BY

SCOTT P. VAUGHN & KANE GILMOUR

WWW.WARBIRDSOFMARS.COM

www.ingramcontent.com/pod-product-compliance
Lightning Source LLC
Chambersburg PA
CBHW030827020726
47499CB00006B/2108